TALES OF YESTERYEAR

Also by Louis Auchincloss
in Thorndike Large Print®

The Book Class
Honorable Men
Diary of a Yuppie
Skinny Island: More Tales of Manhattan

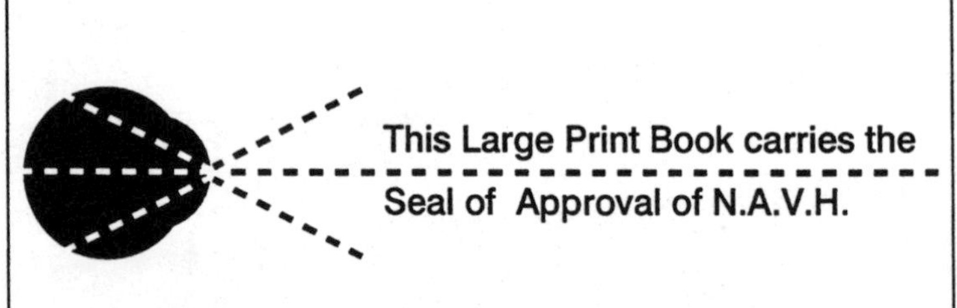

TALES OF YESTERYEAR

Louis Auchincloss

Thorndike Press • Thorndike, Maine

Published in 1994 by arrangement with Houghton Mifflin Company.

Thorndike Large Print ® Basic Series.

The tree indicium is a trademark of Thorndike Press.

The text of this Large Print edition is unabridged.
Other aspects of the book may vary from the original edition.

Set in 16 pt. News Plantin by Rick Gundberg.

Printed in the United States on acid-free, high opacity paper. ♾

Library of Congress Cataloging in Publication Data

Auchincloss, Louis.
Tales of yesteryear / Louis Auchincloss.
p. cm.
ISBN 0-7862-0235-1 (alk. paper : lg. print)
1. Upper classes — United States — Fiction. 2. Large type books. I. Title.
[PS3501.U25T35 1994b]
813'.54—dc20 94-4250

FOR SCHUYLER CHAPIN
AND IN MEMORY OF BETTY

Contents

The Man of Good Will

1

Seth Middleton was more content at noon at his club, the Patroons, more at his ease, more in symbiotic relationship with the small portion of human society in which his lot had been cast, than in the semiretirement of his Wall Street law office or even in his beloved rose garden high over the grey waters of Cold Spring Harbor, in Long Island, where he could sit and play (a harmless old man's game) the benevolent, twinkling oracle to visiting grandchildren, interrupted, only when he waxed too exuberant, by Marjorie's dry put-downs. Such a preference for his fraternity, he would insist, hardly made him a male chauvinist. It was simply, was it not, that there was an unduplicatable camaraderie among those of his male contemporaries (or near contemporaries, as the former, in their seventies, were tending to drop away) who shared, more or less, his own general philosophy and outlook?

"The real thing," Marjorie had once pointed out to their daughters, "is that your father is worshipped at the Patroons. It's the kind of adulation no man can get from a woman unless she's a dunce or a hypocrite, or both."

Seth had always been aware that his wife saw him with unclouded eyes, and he was grateful that such asperities were mercifully rare, catching him though they did at unguarded moments, as if on a scamper down the corridor from the bathroom clad only in a towel. And deeply devoted husband as he was, he could still be secretly pleased that Marjorie could never cross the threshhold of the Patroons except on ladies' night.

Of course there were already, in these turbulent 'sixties, voices being raised in favor of the admission of women to the club, and while he had some sympathy with the argument that the other sex might be deprived of professional opportunities by its exclusion from certain male enclaves, he insisted that the Patroons did no business at all behind their protective walls, that theirs was simply a place where gentlemen of intellectual tastes could meet in the cool, dark, leathery atmosphere of frayed furniture and much thumbed periodicals, under Victorian genre paintings and dusky examples of the Hudson School, with a freedom hardly compatible with the higher decibels, the brisker interchange and even the admittedly better taste of women. Was it a sin to hold that each sex had something special to contribute to its members in occasional isolation? Certainly Marjorie had no wish to see *him* in her beloved Cosmopolitan Club.

But, alas, what sort of greeting would he get this day at noon, on this fine spring day in the third year of the grisly conflict in Viet Nam, from his cohorts gathered at the round table for the preprandial libation, after the *Times*'s article on Mark's comments on his forthcoming graduation from his Connecticut college?

"Don't go to the club today, dear," Marjorie had urged him.

But he had felt it a duty. These men looked to him for candor, for reassurance, for a touching of hands in the darkening twilight of old age. Did he not look to them for the same? As he took his seat and picked up the gin cocktail which Eric, the bartender, had mixed as soon as he spotted Seth's mound of grey hair rising on the stairway below, he noted a certain quickening in the muttered welcome around the board. He waited.

"Well, your grandson certainly made us sit up this morning, Seth! I assume it was only the pyrotechnics of youth."

"I wouldn't worry about it, Seth," said another. "My wife has a young nephew who talks the same way. It's all for publicity. What is it that Canadian guy, McLuhan, says? Truth is what people think at a particular time? Not what they do. Nothing actually ever *happens.*"

"I'm sorry, gentlemen," came a third voice. "I haven't seen the paper today. What did Seth's grandson say? Or do? Or what are we supposed to think he did?"

Seth turned benignly to the last questioner. "It was Mark Storey, my daughter Angelica's son. My only male grandchild, in fact. He's 'agin' everything. But he's a bright kid, and handsome, too; flashy-eyed, raven-haired, very attractive to the girls. A *Times* roving reporter has been doing pieces on New England graduating classes. He interviewed Mark and others at his fraternity. There must have been quite a crowd there and a lot of drinking, I guess. And pot, too. Anyway, when he asked Mark what he intended to do after graduation, he said he wanted to kill himself."

There was a silence around the table.

"Just bluff, wasn't it, Seth?"

Seth nodded slowly. "One must assume so. The reporter did. He didn't take Mark seriously. He even made a joke of it, and some of Mark's fraternity mates struck the same note. It was a bit like a crowd chanting 'Jump! Jump!' to the man on the window ledge. I didn't like that, of course, but I have a lot of faith in Mark. Even if he does call me the 'bought mouthpiece of the vested interests.' "

"Oh, no! Not to your face, surely?"

"Oh, yes, and that's when he's being complimentary. I wouldn't care to repeat some of his other descriptions here." Seth turned now to Ralph Sachs, the pundit of *Everywhere* magazine. "Why are they so down on us, Ralph?"

"Because they think we're mad. The imperialist in the past wanted to conquer the world. Today he wants to blow it up. As they see it, anyway."

Seth rubbed his brow in perplexity. "The war may be a mistake, but I'm damned if I see why it's imperialistic. We don't want anything in either Viet Nam. We want the south to be free, that's all. Why is that a crime?"

"Who said a blunder was worse?"

And then they all turned, with evident relief, from the dangerous topic of Mark to the less dangerous one of the war, and the same old differing points of view were all presented, from escalation to de-escalation, with an escalating sharpness quite uncharacteristic of the usual club discussions.

But Seth was not listening. He was thinking of Mark. He believed that the war had merely intensified in the young man a state of anxiety which had long preceded it. Mark had already been on drugs when it began; he had actually been kicked out of Chelton School for that. And even before the drugs he had insisted on seeing contemporary society as a moral wasteland.

Angelica and her husband, Sam, had long despaired of Mark, and the sombre youth, enfranchised by a small trust fund, had seemed only too grimly satisfied at the pass to which he had brought them. Indeed, it sometimes appeared to be only his grandfather's persistent efforts to reason with him, Seth's refusal to accept the boy's secession from society, that kept Mark in touch with his family at all. But why, Seth wondered with a catch at his heart so painful that he wondered for a moment if he had betrayed himself to the chattering table, should it have been ordained that he, in his senescence, should still find rewards in living in a world where a healthy young man found only dust and ashes?

He could suddenly sit there no longer. They were gabbling like old fools, wrangling over a destiny that the contemptuous young had abandoned to them. With a brusqueness unlike him, he quit the table and then the club.

At home he found Marjorie in the front hall, turning over the mail. He sought immediate comfort in the firm stockiness of her short figure, in the uncompromising sobriety of her dress, even in the gleam of scalp under her thinning grey hair. She had none of his doubts, or if she did, she hid them. She came from Boston; indeed, she had never left it. She always tried to stand between her husband and the inevitable disillusionment which awaited what she regarded as his weak male optimism.

"That was a quick lunch."

"You were right. I shouldn't have gone there. Can I have a sandwich here?"

"Nellie will make you one. I'm going out." She put on her hat without looking at herself in the hall mirror. "Try not to fret, dear. It won't help you. *Or* Mark."

"Marjorie, I'm grateful to you."

"Whatever for?"

"For never having once, in all these years, said, 'I told you so.' "

"About what, for heaven's sake?"

Ah, but that session at the club had really pushed him far! He was ready for anything now. "About my shoving poor Sam into Angelica's calculated embrace."

"Oh, Lordy me!" But her tone was more of impatience than shock. "What do you think I am, a fiend? Anyway, they've been good enough for each other. It wasn't that bad a match. And you can't blame Mark on his parents."

"I don't. I blame him on *me*. But I keep

reminding myself that he may have inherited at least some part of your character. *That* should get him through, if nothing else does."

"Speriamo!"

"And Marjorie. I think I'll drive up to Connecticut this Sunday and lunch with him."

He not infrequently went up to the little town of Mark's college and took him out for a good lunch at a local inn.

"I wouldn't if I were you. I'd leave the boy alone. To show him you weren't scared. But then I'm not you."

And now she did leave. Watching her descend the brownstone stoop, he was horribly afraid that what she was really thinking was that his basic mistake had been in preventing Angelica from aborting Mark. But at least she would never say it.

2

On his Sunday visits to Mark, Seth liked to start early enough to arrive in time for the morning service in the college chapel. There was no idea, of course, of Mark's joining him. He preferred anyway to be alone in church.

He was an Episcopalian. It was not that he regarded its creed as the true one; he credited no faith as a sole key to mysteries into which he had no curiosity to penetrate. But its rites were measured, soothing and colorful; he loved the melodious phrases of the old Jacobean bishops: "Hear what comfortable words our saviour Christ saith unto all who truly turn to him," or "In my Father's house are many mansions; if it were not so I would have told you." Indeed, he was not ashamed to own that such faith as he had might not survive the least revision of the King James version.

And as his own father, the beloved old editor of a famed family periodical, had liked to point out, Episcopalianism was not stained by any spasms of vulgar evangelism, nor did its ministers, like Catholic priests, intrude upon your private life with tiresome and even impudent comminations. It rather provided a ceremony for rest and *receuillement* at the end of a busy week, a welcome caesura for the proper scanning of a line in the good life.

But that morning nothing seemed to work. The hymns crawled with laudations. What was this greedy deity whose vanity had to be soothed with eternal hosannas? And the young minister's sermon was disquietingly mystical. He spoke eerily of a "union with God." How was it possible, Seth thought fretfully, for any human being to derive satisfaction from the concept of such a blending, presumably at the sacrifice of his own personality? He had always shied away from thoughts of an afterlife. The idea of extinction was obnoxious enough, but that of survival was in some ways worse. For might there not be accounts to be settled? Why should he, unlike millions, have been allowed with impunity to enjoy so long and so intensely his habitation of the planet Earth?

Was something like that not on Mark's mind?

He rose and left the church. He found his grandson reading alone in his pleasant dormitory single room, hung with travel posters of French cathedrals and châteaux. Mark never betrayed pleasure or even surprise at his ancestor's arrival. He treated Seth as casually as he would have a classmate dropping in for a chat.

"What's the book?"

"*Sebastian van Storck.* By Walter Pater. Do you know it?" When Seth shook his head, Mark proceeded, with his customary deliberation, to expound the plot. It involved a young Dutch aristocrat of the seventeenth century who believed that the only purpose in life was in its extinction, that the live spirit in all forms of finite existence was doomed at last to be snuffed out, giving place to nullity.

Mark then read this passage aloud:

" 'For him, Sebastian, that one abstract being was as the pale arctic sun, disclosing itself over the dead level of a glacial, a barren and absolutely lonely sea. The liverly purpose of life had been frozen out of it. What he must admire, and love if he could, was "equilibrium," the void, the *tabula rasa,* into which, through all those apparent energies of man and nature which, in truth, are but forces of disintegration, the world was really settling.' "

"But even if all that is true," Seth protested with a shudder, "shouldn't we try to enjoy ourselves in the meantime?"

"But, Grandpa, don't you *see?* That's just what I *am* doing! My enjoyment is in seeing the truth. Even if I'm the only one who does. What would *not* be enjoyable would be to believe that man was wonderful, noble, great, if you will, and yet *still* doomed to extinction."

"So that those of us who believe in the greatness of man — or at least in his potential greatness — and who try to persuade others to believe in it, are doing them no favor?"

"That's how I see it, yes."

"And that's how you see me when I come up here? As an officious proselytizer?"

"Oh, I don't say you're officious. But you're certainly a proselytizer, Grandpa. One of the worst. You're always trying to put a fair face on things. A false face. I prefer the skull." He grinned. "The grinning skull!"

"How do I put a false face on things?"

"Look, Grandpa. Let's not go on with this. I don't want to hurt you. What's the use of that?"

"But I *want* to find out. Isn't that right, by your standards? Isn't that facing the truth?"

Mark reflected and at last nodded. "Very well. If you really want to know. Remember. You asked for it. Let me put it this way." Again he paused to think. "You're always cleaning things up. You think your rich clients make up for their piracy by creating foundations. You believe that letting witnesses tell lies or semi-lies in a courtroom is the best way of finding out truth. And of course you maintain that any amount of blowing up of other nations is justified if its purpose is to bring down dictators. And so you go, on and on, until you've half-convinced yourself you've conquered the ape in man!"

Seth found himself reflecting how far the young man had gone in bridging the double generational gap. It was as if he and Mark were standing on a broad plain with nothing, even equality, between them.

"But, my dear boy, these ideas are all mere approximations. Rough tools, if you will, to build some kind of shelter against bleak, cold facts. I never claimed to have all the answers."

"I realize that, Grandpa. But I'm talking about your effect on other people. You're always urging them to scramble into one of your shelters."

"Is it so great to be out in the cold?"

"It's honest, anyway."

"And can't it be honest to be happy? Look, Mark. Why not count your blessings, for a change? No, I don't care if I sound old hat. You're young and healthy and well-to-do. And you're a citizen of the richest and most democratic nation on earth."

"Whose founding father was a slaveholder."

"But whose real father was Lincoln."

"There you go, Grandpa. There's your old washing machine at work again."

"Your mother used to talk like that. But she came to terms with life."

"You mean by giving up living. For cards and clothes and dinner parties."

"You're hard on her. You can't know as I did what she saved herself from. She was the most reckless debutante of her year. There was something almost suicidal in the way she drank and carried on. And then along came your father and changed her whole life. Believe me, it was better."

"Sam Storey changed plenty of things, I gather. Including the basic character of your and his law firm. Was that better, too, Grandpa? I know you hated it! From the summer I worked there. One of the old guard lawyers told me what a different place it had been in your day. Less hard-boiled."

"I was afraid you'd say it was more honest to be hard-boiled." Seth was touched by this hint of the boy's sympathy with what had been his own disillusionment. Might that sympathy not be the only hold anyone still had on him? "But why did you refer to your father that way? By his name, I mean. Is that some new fashion of the emancipated son?"

"No." Mark rose and went to the window. The back that he turned to Seth was suddenly defiant. "I referred to him that way because he's *not* my father." He allowed a silence to underscore the point. "Don't pretend to be surprised, Grandpa. He said you knew all about it."

Seth's lips and tongue were dry, his mind an echoing chamber. Ever since the break between Mark and his parents he had been dreading that his son-in-law would be goaded into this revelation. But he hadn't been able to bring himself to believe that Sam would be capable of such cruelty. "Oh, my poor boy," he muttered at last.

"But I'm not your poor boy." Mark's tone was harsher now. "I'm apparently the poor boy of the louse who left Mother in the condition in which the generous Mr. Storey condescended to accept her."

"Sam really loved your mother, Mark. I'll not take that from him. When did he tell you this?"

"Does it matter? A couple of weeks ago."

"Was that why you . . ."

"Told that reporter I wanted to kill myself? Not entirely. But the touch of cheap melodrama that Mr. Storey added to my bio made a sudden finale seem all the more appropriate."

"Whatever could have induced your . . . induced Sam to do anything so horrible as spring that on you?"

"Oh, he had cause." Mark now resumed his seat and fixed feverish eyes on his grandfather. "He came up here to talk to me about the draft. He was afraid I was going to do something that would disgrace the family. We hadn't talked in almost a year, and the conversation got heated. He called me a coward and a Red. He said I was afraid to fight and that he was ashamed of me. I said I was ashamed of *him,* ashamed to be his son. That was when he blew his top and told me I wasn't. But why should I really care? Maybe I'm just as glad not to be. I don't think I even care *who* my real father was. I suppose you know."

Seth slowly nodded. "He's dead. He died of a brain tumor when he was only thirty. So you wouldn't have had him as a father for long, in any event."

"Did I miss much?"

"He was certainly an intelligent man."

"But a louse. I get it. Why wouldn't he marry Mother?"

Seth pondered this for a few moments, rather desperately. But surely in these dark questions truth was the only guide he now had. "Because he wasn't sure you were his child."

Mark's laugh was jeering. "She really lived it up, didn't she?"

"Not that much. I believe his suspicions were unjust."

"But anyway, nobody wanted me, did they? Why didn't she have an abortion?"

"Because somebody *did* want you."

"Who, for God's sake?"

"I did. You might as well have the full story. Sam had been putting every penny he could get his hands on into the stock of a client drug company. He had worked on its account since its organization and was convinced it had a booming future."

"Burchwald? And of course it did."

"Indeed it did. It made his fortune. But it was still a gamble back then and he had no capital. He and your mother had been planning to marry after a discreet abortion. He was crazy about her, but he was even crazier about Burchwald. So I offered them a wedding gift of a hundred thousand dollars if they would marry and have you. He talked your mother into it, and there we were."

Mark had jumped to his feet in an agony of nerves. "And you were rich enough to do that? Back then?"

"It was a good chunk of my capital. Your grandmother, I must say, was very understanding."

"But *why,* Grandpa? Why did you care?"

"Because I wanted *you,* my boy. I wanted you more than anything I'd ever wanted in my life."

"But you couldn't have known I'd be a boy."

"I didn't care. I wanted you. That fetus, if you like."

"I'm not sure I like any part of it." He paced the room excitedly as he figured it out. "You wanted a grandchild. And I suppose you knew already that Aunt Olive couldn't have one. But Mother could have had more children. And of course she did."

"One more. But that's not the point. I tell you, I wanted *you.* Don't ask me why. I don't know."

Mark shook his head ruefully. "Poor Grandpa. Look what you got for your money. You'd better have kept it. Except, of course, Sam Storey made millions with it."

"I'm very happy with what I got." Seth paused until he was sure his tone would be as grave as he intended it should be. "You see I've cared for you, Mark, since before you were born. I've cared for you more than I've cared for any other human being in my life. Even, God forgive me, than your grandmother, and I've cared for her very much."

"But, Grandpa, that's crazy!" He stopped pacing to scratch his scalp with both hands. "You're just saying that because you want me to feel loved. You're afraid I might do myself in if I'm not!"

"Yes, I'm saying it to keep you from doing anything wild," Seth conceded. "But it's still true. Why shouldn't you know that you owe your life to me? And that your life is necessary to my happiness? Maybe to my own life? If the truth will help to save you, then there's the truth!"

"You're blackmailing me, Grandpa! You're trying to blackmail me into living!"

"Damn right I am. And now enough of this. As the villain in *The Green Bay Tree* says just before the heroine shoots him, 'Everything points to a very good lunch.' Shall we adjourn to the inn?"

"No. You go. You've given me too much to think about."

"I'll go if you promise me something."

"Not to blow my brains out? I promise."

Seth decided it was the wise thing to leave Mark to himself. When he got back to New York that evening he found that Marjorie, who had spent the day with Angelica, had learned from her daughter of Sam's injudicious revelation. She approved of the way Seth had handled the situation, summing the matter up in her dry factual way, which reminded him uncomfortably of his morning thoughts in church.

"Mark basically envies you, my dear. I think many young people do. Because having been born where you were, when you were and *who* you were made you the luckiest man in the world. You've had it all, Seth. Success, love and the sense of being a thinking and contributing man. What does it matter even if Mark's black cosmos is true?"

3

Seth's had indeed been a good life, the first fifty years of it anyway, and how much more could any man expect?

When, at twenty-seven, a hefty six-footer with shaggy auburn hair and a craggy grin which usually assured him of a friendly reception, he accepted a job at Pettibone & Gates, he had already tried his hand at several trades. He had published, with mild success, a historical novel about Nathan Hale; he had edited, with less success, a liberal journal; he had run and lost a race for a seat in the New York State Assembly; and he had attended Columbia Law School, graduating first in his class. He had then hung out a lone shingle in Maiden Lane and won a series of lawsuits for indigent plaintiffs against grudging insurance companies. Lewis Pettibone, whom he had defeated in the last of these, impressed with his forensic talent, had sought him out and, in Seth's humorous phrase, "bought" him.

The Pettibone firm numbered some dozen

lawyers, half of them partners and half clerks, between whom a moderate familiarity existed, checked, but only temporarily, by outbursts of semi-simulated wrath on the part of the former and semi-simulated awe on that of the latter. But what really united the firm was an old-fashioned veneration for their profession, in the practice of which they deemed wit and scholarship quite as necessary as accuracy and toil, and there seemed to be a cordial agreement among all, even the lowest paid, that the elegances of life were as little as possible to be neglected, that a good Saturday night dinner should be saved up for and followed by Caruso and Farrar at the Met, that a brief could be improved by literary or even Latin quotations, and that the lowest form of life was the attorney who joined a country club and played golf to put himself in the way of retainers.

The firm, which had become Middleton & Gates after Pettibone's retirement, swelled considerably under Seth's management, and a move was necessitated to larger quarters on Wall Street, but he was determined that it should never become what he called a "corporation law factory." He made a great point of preserving as much as possible the friendly give-and-take of the earlier time, and as most of the major clients were his, he was able to impose his will — or his benevolent philosophy, as he preferred to call it — on younger partners who might have dreamed of one day rivaling the Cravath or Davis Polk firms.

Sam Storey became Seth's indispensable right arm at the office. He had been made a member of the firm when still under thirty, and five years later, in 1945, he was generally considered the heir presumptive of the senior partner. He even looked the part of the young Yankee executive. With blond hair and square chin and serious, very serious blue-grey eyes, he might have been drawn by the patriotic hand of Howard Chandler Christie. And he seemed to want nothing better in life than to try cases with Seth Middleton. He was always ready for work and more work; he never looked tired or bored, and his dark, form-fitting suits rarely showed a wrinkle. Sam in Seth's eyes was perfect.

Of course, Seth was not a fool. He knew that Sam knew precisely what he was worth to Seth. Sam did not have to hint awkwardly, like other juniors, that he'd like to know just where he stood in the firm; he was confident that with any luck and a proper play of his hand, and always keeping a weather eye out for competition, he would one day sit in Seth's chair. Seth did not mind this; he liked a young man to be realistic, even a bit hard-headed, and besides, might not such qualities act as occasional checks to his own sometimes too high-flung ideals?

Naturally, his dream would have been a match between Sam and one of his two daughters. Olive was too simple and plain to be a candidate, and she already had her own plain beau, whom she adored, but the lovely and giddy Angelica might well lure Sam on the theory of opposites attracting, and Seth invited his younger partner to spend a couple of weekends in Cold Spring Harbor. It didn't work. Angelica, a party-obsessed eighteen, would have found any serious lawyer a bore, and Sam proved no exception. Though at first intrigued, he appeared, by the end of the second visit, to have accepted her attitude as final. It was therefore with no idea of romance in mind that Seth, a year later, tried to enlist his junior partner's services in the job of persuading Angelica to overcome her distaste for college.

So are the great events of our lives shaped.

"I wish you'd at least talk to the girl about it," Seth ended his plea. He and Sam were lunching at his downtown club. "Why don't you take her out for dinner? Let it be on me. Any fancy bistro you choose. You might be able to drum some sense into that woolly head of hers."

The immediacy of his companion's interest surprised Seth. "What makes you think she'd listen to *me?*"

"Well, of course, she thinks I'm Methusaleh. But a young fellow like you who's already making a name for himself —"

"Angelica's never shown the slightest interest in me," Sam interrupted sharply. "Not on either of those weekends you were kind enough to ask me to. I was just an adjunct of the paternal office. Boring. Hardly worth speaking to."

Seth noted the anger in Sam's tone. "That was probably because she associated you with me. But if you called her on your own, you might get a different reaction. The callow youths she sees can't compete with a real man."

"Are you serious, Mr. M?"

"Totally serious."

"Haven't I heard she has a steady beau? Why doesn't *he* talk to her?"

"If there's anything steady about Angelica, I've yet to hear about it."

Sam stared down at the table. "You're not setting me up for a kick in the pants?"

"Why should I want to do that?"

"Oh, you wouldn't want to, of course. But she might think it a lark on a rainy day, when there was nothing else to do, to make an ass of her old man's partner. Anyway, thank you very much, I'm not going to give her the chance."

"Sorry I brought the matter up," Seth responded, and they returned to their earlier discussion of an antitrust case. But that night when he arrived home Marjorie had some startling news for him.

"What do you think? Angelica's gone out with Sam Storey. Did you put him up to it?"

"And if I did?"

"I thought you were so fond of that young man."

"Well, Angelica's not going to eat him, is she?"

"Isn't she? What is she up to, anyway? He was smitten by her when he was down in the country, and she wouldn't give him the time of day."

"*Smitten?* You never told me that."

"I should have thought it was perfectly obvious. I saw no future in it and put it out of my mind. But I happened to be in the hall when he telephoned, and I heard her exclamation of surprise. Then she became almost flirty."

"Can't a girl change her mind? Maybe she's been brooding about him and couldn't imagine he'd ever call after the way she treated him."

"She's been brooding about something, that's for sure."

4

Seth had never had the courage to probe too deeply into the mind of his daughter Angelica, which was why she liked him the little she did. Her mother *had,* which was why Angelica hated her.

This animosity first crystallized in Angelica's fourteenth year, over the episode of Eva Pennington's birthday party. Eva was in Angelica's class at the Brearley School, a fat, plain, noisy girl with a tendency to be overaffectionate and to push classmates into corners to tell them surprisingly dirty jokes, which she picked up God knows where. She lived with a pretty widowed mother, known to be on her "uppers," who supplemented a meagre income by working as assistant manager of a fashionable men's club. Eva was not "the thing" to Angelica's little set, and she had not asked Eva to her own birthday party.

Angelica's mother had put in a plea for Eva.

"Aren't you going to ask the little Pennington girl?"

"*Little!*" was Angelica's scornful retort. "I am not!"

"I've an idea that child has a rather hard time. I'm sure her mother would appreciate it if she were asked."

"Is my party for her mother, or is it for me?"

"Very well, Angelica, you may ask whom you wish."

But the following fall Mrs. Pennington pulled off the great coup of her marriage to Alfred Starr, the old bachelor president of the club where she worked, and Eva was legally adopted by the largest holder of railroad securities in the nation. When her mother gave *her* a birthday party in the old Starr mansion on upper Fifth Avenue, Eva invited her whole class, including, of course, Angelica. The latter accepted, but foreseeing trouble, she did not tell her mother.

On the afternoon of the party, however, Marjorie Middleton happened to be coming home just as Angelica, duly arrayed, was leaving with her nurse. When her daughter failed at once to answer her question of where she was bound, the nurse replied for her. "To Mrs. Starr's, ma'am. The children's birthday party I mentioned to you this morning."

"Ah, yes, Ellen. But I hadn't taken in whose. I'm afraid you'll have to go upstairs and change, Angelica. I'll telephone Mrs. Starr and say you have a cold. Fortunately it's Friday, so the weekend will give you time to have recovered before you see Eva at school on Monday."

Angelica felt a hot compression in her chest which for a moment choked her response. Then she erupted. "Why?" she screamed. "Why, why, *why?*"

Her mother surveyed her coolly. "You know perfectly well why. You wouldn't ask Eva to your party. Of course you can't go to hers."

"But she's asked the whole class!"

"What difference does that make? You must learn that you cannot accept things from people unless you're willing to give them the same."

"But I'm quite willing to ask Eva to any party of mine!"

"You are *now,* I see. And I'm afraid that the reason for your change of attitude is not a very attractive one. However, *after* you have asked Eva here, then you will be free to go to her place. But today is out of the question."

"I doubt if Eva would want to set foot now in a shabby old brownstone like ours!"

But this shot fell way short. "It's not in the least shabby, though maybe it could do with a bit of redecoration. But that's neither here nor there. I'm sure Eva will be glad to come here. I doubt she's the snob that some little girls I know seem to be."

"I hate you, I hate you, I hate you!"

"Ellen, take this naughty girl upstairs and put her to bed, will you please? I'll ask her father to have a little chat with her in the morning. The one thing I will not put up with is a vulgar child."

Angelica had little difficulty with her father in the morning; she could always handle *him.* But the conflict with her mother had been permanently defined. So far, anyway, as Eva Pennington was concerned, the incident proved actually beneficial to Angelica's social ambitions. Mrs. Starr sent flowers to her supposed sick bed, and Eva agreed to come to supper with her the very next week, showing no disdain of simple brownstone. Indeed, the two girls soon became such bosom friends that Angelica was invited to go cruising with the Starrs on their great steam yacht, the *Arethusa*, the following summer. Marjorie had her doubts about allowing Angelica to accept, but Seth, desperately cajoled by his younger daughter, persuaded his wife to approve.

Marjorie had described her daughter as *vulgar,* and the word had widened the gulf between them to impassability. It was not simply that Angelica rejected the term as applied to herself; she regarded such application as outrageous hypocrisy on her mother's part. For why did they live cheek by jowl in both town and country with richer neighbors? Why were she and her sister sent to private schools and summer camps with the children of the same? Why were they listed in the *Social Register* and why did her mother belong to the Cosmopolitan Club and her father to the Union as well as the Patroons? Why did so many of the latter's funny stories deal with the drolleries of his wealthiest clients? What was the point of their whole existence unless it was to climb to the very apex of the social pyramid, which, like Everest, was always so challengingly "there"?

Of course, Angelica knew the counterarguments well enough. She couldn't remember a time when they hadn't been dinned in her ears. They were "nice" people; that was always the point. Mother and the girls were "ladies" and Daddy was a "gentleman," and ladies and gentlemen, if properly raised, should be able to handle any amount of pitch without becoming defiled, indeed, without having to wash their hands. They didn't spend their summers on Long Island's north shore because it was a social resort. Heaven forbid! They went there because it was a good commute for Daddy and because of the good sailing. And as for Daddy's clients, well, wasn't a lawyer supposed to serve those who knocked at his door, and wasn't it inevitable that men of large means should use their money to avail themselves of his undoubted expertise?

Yes, yes, yes, but still! The mere fact that such a goose as her older sister should have bought the whole kit and caboodle, that Olive in her gushing enthusiasm, in her demonstrative pawing of both parents (but much more particularly Daddy), should take so for granted that their father, the font of kindly wisdom and benign idealism, should provide her with a new Eden in which she could innocently prance and prattle until some young counterpart of himself should carry her off to the oo-la-la of a blissful marriage, was enough to make her younger sibling vomit. Yet so strong and sure was the fabric of the parental launching machine that even such a ninny as Olive might indeed end up with an adequately respectable spouse.

But only adequately. For her, Angelica, greater things had to be in store. She carefully cultivated her differences from her sister. If the latter was open-hearted, she would be subtle, mysterious; if Olive was gleeful, she would be reserved, sceptical, of generally finer palate. She adopted at an early age the pose of the sophisticated, poised, diminutive creature, demure, loving to dress up her dolls, emulating any stylish lady who swept into her ken, and uttering little cries of affection whose very innocent insincerity and guile could be a part of their charm. She was not destined to be a beauty, as her small but pronounced features tended to merge too closely together and her movements verged on the jerky, but she was at least "prettifiable," and she managed to give a certain style, a sort of "chic" to her occasional awkwardness, a handsome boldness to her profile (her best feature, always emphasized) and something like warmth to an unexpectedly rumbling laugh. She grew up into a young woman whom her father and enough young men found interesting. Her mother, of course, was never taken in. The trouble with Marjorie Middleton as a parent was not that she didn't love her children, but that she *saw* them.

The major crisis in the Middleton family arose over the question of Angelica's debutante party. Seth had formulated a series of what he liked to term "amiable bribes" to his daughters. One was that a five-thousand-dollar check would be found on the breakfast plate of each on her twenty-first birthday if she should have abstained from hard liquor until that date. Another twenty-five hundred would be added if she had also not smoked.

And a third "bribe" was that each girl, at eighteen, would be offered the choice between a coming-out party and a trip to Europe. Olive had opted for the trip, and her father was so pleased at this evidence of a serious turn of mind that he had thrown in the party as well, and she had come out at a big supper dance at Cold Spring Harbor with a marquee, a popular jazz orchestra, gallons of champagne and the usual number of intoxicated stag crashers.

When it came to Angelica's turn, however, the preliminary discussion between her and her parents took a very different direction.

"I'm quite aware, Daddy, that if I act the good little girl, like Olive, I can have the trip *and* the party. But if I choose the party, does it mean I get neither?"

"Now what makes you think I'd play you a trick like that?"

"Oh, just because."

"Because what?"

Angelica's glance at her mother was challenging. "Because Mother always thinks I'm so worldly."

"And you're not?" Marjorie responded. "Tell me you're not, dear, and I'll believe you."

"I take the world as I find it. I didn't make it, Mother."

"I take it anyway," Seth intervened hastily,

"that you *do* want the party. That's all right. You shall have it. But I confess that I wonder a little why you find it so important. Aren't these big deb bashes becoming anachronistic?"

"They'll last my time. And my time is what I've got. I've a much better chance of finding the right husband on the dance floor than in some stupid girls' college."

"And what, pray, do you consider the 'right' husband? One of those callow young drunks who crash all the parties these days?"

"They aren't all that, Daddy. A girl can pick and choose. There'll be plenty of eligible young men at my party. I'll see to that."

"Eligible?"

"What Angelica means by eligible, Seth, is a man who can support her in the style to which she has every intention of becoming accustomed."

"Well, what's wrong with that, Mother? That's what plenty of girls want, though they're very careful not to say so. You're always penalizing me for honesty."

"Is it really honesty, Angelica, dear?" Her father was very earnest now. "I hope at Vassar you may straighten out some of your more extreme ideas."

"I'm not going to Vassar."

"But you've been accepted!"

"Well, not for a year, anyway. I want to

do this debutante thing right if I do it at all. Every dance, every house party, the works. When the year's over, well, then we'll see about college."

Seth and Marjorie exchanged a long look, after which Marjorie, as if by tacit agreement, took the lead.

"I think we should make the party conditional on your matriculating at Vassar this coming fall."

Angelica jumped to her feet, her eyes ablaze. "But Daddy promised me, Mother! He can't go back on it now!"

"Suppose we agree that if you'll take some courses at Columbia, we'll go ahead with the party?" Seth suggested.

Marjorie at this rose to leave the room. "I'm not going to stay and watch you crumble into utter defeat, Seth."

Angelica in the following season went out and about the town even more than she had threatened. Her name appeared in society columns with a frequency that caused Seth to suspect she was using a publicity agent, presumably paid for by Eva Pennington. And she was wearing dresses evidently from the same source, as her allowance would never have covered such quality and variety. But her shrill "Can't I even accept a present from a friend?"

was all the answer that his inquiries brought, and Marjorie warned him not to probe too far.

"That Pennington girl has a hopeless crush on her. She wants her to come and live with her at the Starrs'. How would *that* look? Never forget that Angelica is eighteen. She can do what she wants. Don't push her too hard!"

Certainly Angelica was taking the fullest advantage of Eva's generosity. While she didn't actually move in with the Starrs, she practically lived at their great houses in New York and Greenwich and aboard the sparkling *Arethusa*. Eva and Eva's mother were enchanted to be towed in the wake of the lively girl who became, if not the most popular, certainly the most publicized debutante of the 1946 season. And, needless to say, no courses were taken at Columbia.

Several young men fell in love or thought they had fallen in love with Angelica, but it was universally observed, and noted by every society columnist, that she had one particularly faithful escort, Jason Lee, Jr., the only son of the senior partner of Lee, Bensonhurst, a major investment banking house on Wall Street.

Jason was already working in his father's firm, having graduated from Harvard the previous spring, which made him in debutante eyes vastly superior to the college crowd who composed the bulk of the male guests at dances. He was tall and lanky and had an oblong countenance, a bit too much on the horsey side to be really handsome, and his mocking grey eyes were a touch too close together, but he had a fine, an almost Barrymore profile enhanced by long loose hair, and his harsh, high laugh could dominate any group he found himself in. But then he always chose his own group.

He was supposed to be brilliant, having scraped through college on trots and summaries, virtually memorized at a glance. He professed contempt for learning as pedantry and for most forms of art as showing off. He played no sport but golf, in which he excelled, and no parlor game but bridge, in which he was a champion. He spent money lavishly and boasted that his old man would back him in anything, even if it should break him. But nothing, everyone knew, *could* break his old man. Jason liked to warn his friends, "The only thing that nobody can believe about me is that I'm a son of a bitch."

He and Angelica laughed at the same things, which meant that she laughed at the things he did. He seemed to her the first person she had ever known who saw the world exactly as it was. She allowed him to monopolize her, taking her off the dance floor, where she would really rather have stayed, to sit out on terraces or in conservatories while he languidly discoursed on his views of life.

Jason used the word *vulgar* in a very different sense from her mother's. He regarded *accomplishment* as vulgar if tainted with the least grubbiness of competition.

"Lord Melbourne was so right in what he said about the Order of the Garter," he remarked one evening. "That it had none of the stink of merit. The best things in life come of their own accord, on their own terms. That is, if they come at all. Our real business is to appreciate, not to create."

"But to get anywhere in life, don't you have to invest in something?" Angelica protested, thinking of what her publicity had cost Eva. "Don't you have to build?"

"What do you mean by getting somewhere in life?"

"Oh, I know you're going to accuse me of having middle-class values. But I don't mean just becoming president of your father's firm. Or even of the United States. I mean anything beautifully done. Didn't you tell me you were writing sonnets?"

"I did. I actually dream of composing a perfect one. Even Shakespeare couldn't cope with the final couplet."

"Very well. The perfect sonnet won't just come, will it?"

"I wonder if it mightn't. If I clear my mind of all thought of publication. It's no coincidence that our greatest poet, Emily Dickinson, wouldn't publish in her lifetime."

"Yet you wouldn't have had those poems if she hadn't left them to be printed after her death!"

"Ah, but death caught her unawares. I don't believe she ever intended that. In some ways it would have been a finer thing had they perished with their creator. Unsoiled. Perfect."

"So you believe that instead of taking all the trouble to become a debutante, I should just have *thought* about being one?"

"But, my dear, your case precisely bears out my argument! You had only to appear, and you were the toast of the season."

"There was no 'merit' in it?"

"Perish the thought! There was only you."

Constantly as they saw each other, Jason never made love to her, beyond an occasional good-night kiss, which was really only a brush of the lips. Yet as she well knew, he was known to have had love affairs, "real" affairs, which was not the universal thing (excluding commercial sex) for very young men of that day. And she was only too keenly aware that he had never uttered a word about marriage, which, after all, was the fixed star of her ambition. She didn't suppose that she was "hopelessly" (wasn't that the adverb?) in love with him; indeed, she wasn't sure she was in love with him at all. But she was very sure that he was financially and physically everything she wanted.

At last she ventured to play around the subject.

"Would your wife have to be a virgin?" she challenged him one night. She smiled as she asked the question. He did not as he answered it. "Absolutely."

"But supposing you fell passionately in love with a nice girl, a virtuous girl, if you will, and . . ."

"I do not disdain the term."

"Very well. And let us suppose she was just as much in love with you as you with her, and you were thrown together under circumstances that made you both lose your heads —"

"Pardon me," he interrupted. "I never lose my head."

"All right, but *she* does. She offers herself to you, and you, I suppose, like a gentleman, comply. Would that mean you'd never marry her?"

"Certainly."

Perversely enough, this attitude greatly intensified his physical attraction for her. The idea that he might have no intention of marrying her, that he was cynically biding his time until his charm should have drawn her like a magnet into a bed that she knew in advance would be fatal not only to her marital aspirations but perhaps to her very reputation, began to have a strange fascination for her. What sort of man was this who could so patiently and coldly plan her undoing, showing her every card in his hand, watching her with snake-like eyes and offering not the slightest gesture of endearment as she stripped, helplessly, before him? Or was it only her fantasy? But she was now having restless nights. For once, anyway, she was not bored.

For the parties *had* begun to bore her, even before the end of her first season. Yet she couldn't bear to admit that she might have been wrong and her parents right, and to the latter's dismay, and encouraged by the adoring and ever generous Eva, she refused to consider college and embarked on a second season of revels. By early spring of her first post-debutante year she had exhausted the last grim pleasures of coming out. She had danced untold hours; she had ridden and hunted through uncounted miles of Connecticut, Long Island and New Jersey estates; she had learned the anodyne of liquor, though she never showed its effects. And she and Jason had already become a kind of legend in the worlds of urban night life and rural equestrian pursuits. They were always together now, always in unison in their derision of anything that offered them escape from their trap, like two footnotes in the appendix of a history of the Jazz Age.

"You have taught me something at last," she confessed to him one early morning when they were almost alone in the night club La Rue. "There is nothing I want in society."

"The great Oscar put it well. To be in society is simply a bore. But to be out of it is simply a tragedy."

"Ah, but I'm not at all sure of that. To be out of everything may be precisely what is not a bore."

"You mean to be a little dead birdie?"

"Isn't that what you're headed for?"

"Only in the sense that we all are. I shouldn't mind if the pace at which I live brought me to it faster."

"Certainly I see little point in dallying."

To be naked in his arms and yield him everything he desired — no, more — to thrust herself on him, to possess *him,* with the dark satisfaction of knowing she was forfeiting her last chance of becoming Mrs. Jason Lee, Jr., that she would be kicked out of his bed in the morning like a used whore . . .

"Jason, do you know something?"

"What, my sweet?"

"You're not quite as rotten as you like to think."

"Ah, spare me one illusion."

"Not even one. Because you've converted me. When I first met you I cared desperately about your money. Now I don't give a fig for it."

"You mean, to win you I'd have to give it away?"

"You'd never do that."

"Damn right I wouldn't. What would I be without it?"

"You *do* see that, do you?"

"Of course I see it. Just as I wonder what you would be without your craving for it."

"Yes," she mused, "you *are* intelligent. But I think, after all, it may not be the only thing I crave."

But less than a month after the single night that she spent with Jason she found that she was pregnant, and her instant reaction of searing panic shattered the glass case of her fragile disillusionment with life.

She would of course have to abort the child, but she had no idea how to go about finding a doctor who would do it. Jason was probably more sophisticated in such matters, or at least would know how to find the answer, but she now loathed him, and the realization that he would surely regard any appeal from her, even if he replied with funds and addresses, as a plea for marriage sickened her almost more than the idea of going to her parents.

Of course, there was always the faithful Eva, but how much did she know about such things, and could one be sure that her stepfather, a prudish sort of man, would not, if approached for a goodly sum, suspect something wrong and go straight to the Middletons?

And then the god from the machine, whom she had read about at school in Gilbert Murray's mellifluous translations of Greek tragedy, leaped down upon the darkening stage of her post-debutante career.

She had gone to her room to avoid the trial of a family dinner, giving the usual headache as her excuse, when her sister, Olive, hammered on the door to say there was a man on the phone.

"Who?"

"Well, it's not Jason."

"But who?"

"Oh, a man. Isn't that enough?"

Really, her sister. But when she came out and picked up the telephone on the landing and heard Sam Storey's serious voice asking whether she would go out for dinner with him one night, she wondered for a mad moment if her news had not somehow leaked and if her father's firm were not seeking to help! Sam Storey, who had so bored her . . . but then she remembered very distinctly that she had not bored *him.* Oh, not at all!

She told him that she would be happy to dine with him that very night.

5

Seth could hardly help be aware of how constantly Angelica and Sam were seeing each other, as the latter was no longer available for ordinary night work at the office, but would leave promptly at six, stating that he would be back at midnight and sit at his desk until dawn if a brief required it. And his attitude towards Seth was suddenly much more reserved and formal. It was as if the positions of favorite junior partner and daughter's swain were somehow incompatible. Seth found himself uncomfortable and faintly bewildered. What was it all about? Wasn't marriage to the boss's daughter the happy ending of many an American business saga?

The answer came one morning when Sam strode silently into his office and closed the door behind him.

"There's something I have to tell you, sir." He didn't take a seat, but stood stiffly before Seth's desk. "Your daughter has turned to me for advice. Advice and assistance."

"Well, could she have picked a better man?"

"This is not exactly a legal question, sir."

Seth cleared his face of all pretense of joviality. "I'm listening, Sam."

"Angelica is pregnant. Almost two months pregnant."

Seth stared, incredulous. *Could* it be that she and Sam . . . ? But no. It couldn't be. He bent over his desk, his hands covering his face. After a moment, with a deep sigh, he looked up. "The wretched Lee?"

"I might kill him one day, but that's another matter. Of course, she wants an abortion. I have made the arrangements. I have a doctor cousin who will do it. He's utterly reliable. And he won't take a cent for it. He's a strong believer in a woman's right to her own body. At this stage, he assures me, there's little risk. But of course I had to tell you. Even though Angelica is of age."

"I see." Seth nodded, almost foolishly. "Is

she at home now?"

"No. She's on her way down to Trenton to stay with my married sister. Lily knows all about it and is the soul of kindness. Nothing will be done until you've had a chance to talk to Angelica on the telephone."

"Her mother doesn't know?"

"Her mother knows nothing. Angelica didn't want either of you to know. But I told her that I would have to tell you."

"Thank you, my boy. I must talk to Lee, don't you think?"

Sam's eyes were hard. "Why, in God's name?"

"Because it's his baby, too. Maybe they should marry and have the child. They could be divorced afterwards."

"But Angelica doesn't want the child!"

"I still have to explore that option. A human being's life is at stake."

"Mr. Middleton, I think you'd better leave this matter to your daughter. She has quite made up her mind about it, and nothing you or her mother can do is going to alter the situation. Angelica and I have become very close. I think I'm on my way to understanding her."

"Which is a way, I suppose, of telling me that I don't. Well, I've never claimed to. But help me, my boy, to understand this friendship between you and her. I don't imagine, under the circumstances, that it could be romantic in nature."

"And why not, sir? Am I to hold one slip against a woman? I'm not such a Victorian."

"A slip. I see."

The hard look in Sam's eyes was now more than defiant. It was almost hostile. Seth was suddenly jarred by the old memory of a golden Labrador retriever he had owned a dozen years back, a magnificent and totally loyal beast, which had always obeyed his whistle until the single time when it was pursuing a bitch in heat. What things had Angelica told this young man about her parents?

He rose and walked to the window to look down on the pyramid of steps that crowned the tower of Bankers Trust, an image of the tomb at Halicarnassus. In his daily ruminations over oral arguments his eye would run up and down them. But now his mind reached out to grasp the peak, to hold on to something to keep his imagination from soaring wildy into the ether. Because he didn't *want* this fine young man to be in love with Angelica! Oh, not at all now! And, good God, wouldn't that an hour before have been his dream of dreams?

"Are you telling me you're going to marry Angelica?"

"Of course I'm going to marry Angelica!

If she'll have me. You talk as if she's been disgraced."

"Would you be willing to marry her and let her have the child?"

"That question hasn't arisen, sir!" Sam explained with exasperation. "I've told you, Angelica doesn't want the child. She has no idea of having the child!"

"All right, all right. I'd better go home now and talk to my wife."

"If you disapprove, sir, of my role in this matter, I'll be glad to offer my resignation from the firm. Because, regardless of what you and Mrs. Middleton decide, I am determined to assist Angelica in going through with this."

"I quite understand that. And don't be an ass about resigning. Now get the hell out of here, will you? You've given me enough to think about."

But when he found himself alone, Seth did not at once prepare to leave the office. He paced the room with his fists clenched and then again took up his position before the window and the view of the famous tomb. To his own astonishment he found that he was trembling with indignation. Was it not the ultimate impertinence on Angelica's part, after finding the pleasures of dissipation as idle as any fool could have told her, to turn back to the despised garden of paternal values and pluck for the satisfaction of her jaded appetite its finest rose? And was it a father's duty to stand by and watch her take over the young man to whom he had destined his firm and his law practice, take him over, too, boldy, cynically, without even bothering to conceal her stain? Did she really care for him? Had not Marjorie once warned him that Angelica would one day get back at her mother *through* her father?

And there was another reason, too, that he should not play a passive role in this drama. Of course there was! Why should a child's life be snuffed out to make way for a loveless (at least on her part) marriage? Why should the poor little guiltless product of a careless, perhaps even a drunken copulation pay with its very existence for the rash lust of its giddy parents? Might not even so poor a thing as Jason Lee be persuaded to convince Angelica where his and her duty lay?

He called his secretary to look up Lee's number. When the telephone rang it was Jason himself who answered, and twenty minutes later the tall young man with the pale face and long hair was seated before him, his legs crossed in an attitude of semi-insolence, which, however resolutely rehearsed on his walk over, did not altogether conceal his nervous tension.

Seth came at once to the point.

"I have been told that you are not aware of my daughter's condition. She is pregnant. Do you acknowledge your responsibility? I am not, believe me, sir, waving a shotgun. I am trying to make out what two honest persons should do, faced with such a situation."

"But I am not clear, Mr. Middleton, what the situation is. You ask, do I acknowledge my responsibility. I acknowledge that I *could* be responsible."

"You have the gall to insinuate . . ." Seth paused, disconcerted by the pounding of his heart. But wait, wait. There was more at stake than hating this odious young man. Much more.

Lee did not wait for Seth to recover himself. "To insinuate that there may have been others? Why should I not, considering her behavior? It was you, sir, who asked for this painful interview, so you had better listen to me. Parents don't always know their children as well as they think they do. I know mine don't. Your daughter has some very advanced ideas about the relations of the sexes."

Seth rose to his feet, trembling. "Hold your tongue, sir!"

Lee seemed to be waiting to be struck in the face. But wouldn't violence put him in a stronger position? Seth sank back into his chair.

"If I'm to hold my tongue, Mr. Middleton, this interview has very little point."

"Pray continue, sir."

"Fathers tend to put their daughters on an altar. Your daughter did not want to be put on an altar. She believes in freedoms that you don't. And, as a matter of fact, that *I* don't. Her business is her business, of course. But if marriage is what you're getting at, I don't choose to marry a girl with your daughter's views for the sake of a child that may not be mine."

"But you seduced her, sir!"

"Seduced her!" The wretch actually smiled! "Mr. Middleton, I'm sorry to shock you, but you give me no alternative. When I was staying with the Starrs in Greenwich, she came into my bedroom at night and got into my bed. Now there may be chaste souls who can resist that sort of advance, but I don't happen to be one of them."

Seth stared at the bold face confronting his. Was there a hint of a wink in the eye? Was it possible that this brash creature was appealing to some kind of male alliance between them? "And you expect me to believe that?"

"Ask your daughter. Has she claimed anything else? I suspect she's too proud to lie."

"But you wouldn't marry her?"

"Be fair with me, sir. Would *you* have?"

Seth stifled a groan. "I mean, to save the child."

"Whose child?"

Seth walked now to the door and held it open. Neither said good-bye. Returning to his desk, he sat quiet and almost motionless for a quarter of an hour. Then he reached for the morning *Times* in the scrap basket and turned to the market page. Burchwald Drugs was selling at 105.

6

Mark, Seth's only grandson as it turned out for Olive, though wed, was to have no children, and Angelica only one more, a daughter, Celeste — was born six months after Sam and Angelica married. The friends and relatives had taken for granted that the couple's precipitate nuptials had followed the discovery that their mutual love had been fruitful; few, in 1947, minded *that*. It was the romantic side of Seth's nature, persistent despite repeated rebuffs, which prompted him to view the season of the boy's birth as one of strife, not only among the nations, for the first bleak gusts of the cold war were already stirring, but in the child's own family, as if the gods, like figures in some gaudy baroque painting, were disputing which should be the patron of the mortal babe.

The deal about the Burchwald stock had removed any question of real intimacy between the Middletons and the Storeys. Sam had too deeply resented Seth's intrusion into his and Angelica's private life and too bitterly recalled the greed that had kept him from rejecting it. The two families met on regular occasions, and Seth and Sam, of course, met daily at the office; an exterior friendliness, which perfectly satisfied the Storeys and Marjorie, decently covered the inner cool. It did not, however, satisfy Seth. What he most minded was the tacit but iron rule that the circumstances of Mark's birth could never be mentioned, even in the most private family sessions, and no matter what bearing they might have on any problems the boy might develop. After Jason Lee's premature death Seth began actually to wonder if Sam might not have forgotten or repressed the whole incident. Sam was not, it was true, a demonstratively affectionate father; affection played little role in his life. But it was notable that he made not the slightest difference in his treatment of Mark and Celeste. He was always more like a schoolmaster than a parent.

His infatuation with Angelica had not long survived his discovery that she was not the wronged, redeemed and near heroic woman that he had, prior to marriage, stubbornly maintained her to be. Though Angelica, indeed, had proven a better wife than her father had anticipated, she was still far from the figure on whose pedestal her spouse had so optimistically carved his tribute. But Sam was a realist; he sturdily converted what he had thought to be a love match into a comfortable and useful alliance. Angelica was a great aid to him. A narrowly escaped disgrace had taught her the value of conventional behavior, and she had learned to control both her drinking and her temper. She concentrated her considerable abilities on dress, poise, charm of manner, hospitality and bridge. There was no more gracious young lady of fashion on the East Side of Manhattan.

"Do you suppose there's any real happiness in a life like that?" Seth once asked Marjorie.

"I'm afraid there must be. Why else would so many women aspire to it?"

Most important of all for the Storeys' marital accord, Sam was now making the big money his wife had always felt to be her due.

Not only did his new stock soar in value; his legal income multiplied. For, like many disillusioned husbands, he had converted all of his formidable energy into work. But he did not confine himself, as he largely had before, to the actual practice of his profession, that is, the nitty-gritty of briefs, indentures, prospectuses, contracts, reorganizations and such. He had begun to take over the administration of the firm. He installed all the new business machines, expanded the work force, cultivated and entertained the clients and, strongly backed by the younger partners, achieved a position which, a mere half dozen years after his marriage, obliged Seth to offer him the senior partnership.

Yet had that not always been the older man's goal? True, but there was a difference now. Sam and his "young Turks" had no interest in the kind of amiable, high-minded, loose confederation of kindred souls united in the love of law that had been Seth's ideal. They cared only to be the biggest and most forceful firm in the street, and if to become the architect of the very toughest corporate raids and take-overs was the price of that, they were only too happy to pay it. How Angelica must have been smiling! It *was* her world, after all.

As parents Sam and Angelica were certainly outwardly proper, and even more generous than others of their own rich set. If Celeste, for example, wished to ride, to sing, to draw, to train for ballet, she could count on her mother to engage the best of instructors, and if Mark wanted to shoot or play golf or give large house parties for his friends or even go on an African safari, he could be sure of his father's friendly nod. Sailboats, horses, autos, and even, should he one day aspire to the skies, an airplane, were readily providable.

But if the boy should manifest an undue zeal for a religious sect or for social work (except, say, for a brief counselorship in a summer camp for poor boys) or, perish the thought, for a radical political cause, he would find himself, not banished or even punished, but wholly estranged from his parents for the duration of his apostasy. Their affection was incapable of reaching beyond the confines of the life in which they themselves found comfort and satisfaction.

If Mark had developed inner tensions under this brand of parental discipline, he did not show them in the first seventeen years of his life, unless they could be made out in his constant habit of questioning. He was always inquiring into the nature of things: the gifts people gave him and why, the lessons he was glad enough to learn but for what purpose, the differences between him and his sister and to whose advantage they might be, even the very heaven the minister on Sunday was always talking about and who was in it and who not. He was a serious and sober boy, with manners almost too good and the charm of beautiful dark eyes and a rapt attention. He responded readily to his grandfather's obvious interest in him and rapidly wove a special relationship between them.

The terrible change in Mark came in his last year at Chelton, the preparatory New England school which Sam, himself a graduate, had insisted on his attending. Mark, to everyone's horror and disbelief, was expelled with three other boys for taking and distributing LSD. He insisted violently that he had been unjustly penalized for what he claimed (the school denied it) was a single offense, and he attributed to the publicity that attended the event his failure to get into a major college. Dissatisfied with the small Connecticut institution where he at last matriculated, he fell in with a bad group, and by senior year was experimenting with heroin.

Seth never discovered how much truth there was in Mark's claim of injustice, but he had little doubt that the boy had totally convinced himself of it. The result was appalling. It was as if the finely sensitive nature and reaching intelligence of this charming youth were possessed of no antibodies with which to combat the rapid growth of the fatal virus. It grew until all his humor and wit had been swallowed up in an arid sarcasm, his bright imagination in a sultry suspicion and his natural affections in a childish dislike of the whole world. Like Hamlet he saw life as an unweeded garden grown to seed, but unlike the prince, he did not regard a release from it as the possible gate to further woes. On the contrary, he seemed to take a macabre pleasure in the prospect of personal annihilation.

It came as little surprise to Seth that the perfunctory parental relationship which Sam and Angelica had established with Mark should have crumbled on its first serious test. Sam was particularly unsympathetic.

"Mark's made an utter hash of his academic life and finds himself in a third-rate college with fourth-rate friends. Very well; he's going to have to straighten things out, and only he can do it. I'm staying out of it, Seth. I told Mark he could have all the special tutors he needed to get his grades up. I promised to buy him a Jaguar if he did. If only my tax-obsessed accountant hadn't bullied me into setting up that trust fund for him, I'd have had more of a whip hand. A parent should never give up the power of the purse."

"It's a dubious power, Sam."

"But there are few enough others!"

Seth got little more satisfaction from his talk with Angelica. She became very excited and defensive.

"I have to leave that young man's problems to Sam. I can't handle them, Dad! You should have heard Mark on the telephone when I asked him if he was planning to attend Sam's niece's coming-out party. He was actually obscene! Well, I can assure you, it'll be a month of Sundays before I call *him* again!"

Seth, without telling anyone but Marjorie, had thereupon taken it upon himself to initiate the Sunday visits to Mark's college. Mark had at first shown himself moody and truculent, as if he were waiting for the old man's moralizing to begin, but when Seth convinced him that he had come rather to listen than to preach, he had relaxed and finally begun to open up. Indeed, by the third visit he waxed almost garrulous. His talk was centered, almost obsessively, on the rot in modern society, largely as exemplified in the lives of his parents.

"My father hides his opportunism under a mask of formal benignity. After all, he might want a federal post one day. Yet his cover is hardly necessary. Who's ever going to analyze his underwritings to find that he and his financial clients invest solely in businesses with minimum labor costs? He dreams of a society where the machine will have done away with the labor union. And who will ever pierce the corporate veils of his foreign enterprises to discover the human peonage and slavery on which they rest?"

"My dear boy, you don't take into account that we are at last, for better or worse, one world. Things have got so interwoven that you can hardly drink a glass of orange juice without exploiting some human being somewhere."

"Well, at least I don't revel in it the way he does."

Seth found it impossible to get him off the subject. Mark turned the topic of Sam Storey over and over, peering at it as through a microscope, stripping off layer after layer of Sam's outward nature to get to the inner core of iniquity. There was no act of Sam's now recalled to which Mark did not attribute a sinister or at least a shabby motive. Towards his mother he was more lenient. He treated her with a mild contempt.

"For Mother there's no law of diminishing returns. She thinks two diamond necklaces are twice as much fun as one, and three, three times as much."

Seth had been almost relieved when his daughter and son-in-law finally suspended relations with Mark. He had dreaded what such constant baiting on the boy's part might at last drive Sam to reveal. And now it had happened. He would have to devise some altogether new approach to lighten Mark's dangerously darkening mind. He read the Pater story of which his grandson had spoken and was surprised to find that it ended on a note of hope. The young Dutch aristocrat who yearned for extinction is caught in a sudden flooding of the dikes and loses his life saving a child's. The letter Seth wrote to Mark was one of barely concealed satisfaction.

7

Mark's imminent graduation made the question of the draft a pressing one, which was indeed what had made Sam break their feud for that fateful meeting, and Seth, on his first visit to Connecticut since he learned of that unhappy scene, was determined to discuss the different courses of action that his grandson might take.

Mark had drunk two cocktails at the inn

before their meal; he seemed restless and disturbed.

"Oh, the war, the rotten war," he muttered. "Why must we always discuss it?"

"Because it's there, Mark."

"It doesn't have to be there for me. Maybe it will never be there for me. Or I for it, for that matter."

"What do you mean by *that?*"

"Oh, never mind, Grandpa. Can I have another drink?"

"No, dear boy, you'd better not."

Mark banged his empty glass on the table. "Well, what would *you* do, Grandpa, in my case? Would you go over there and blow up villages? And spatter the rice paddies with the limbs of women and children?"

Seth paused. He looked away from the feverish dark eyes that were clamped on him. It was a fair question. The war had gravely perplexed him. He wondered if perhaps only professional forces should have been used. Were the issues really clear enough to justify a draft? But his heart ached that young people should no longer respect the flag.

"I guess I don't know what I'd do, Mark. I suppose I'd go. And bomb the villages, as you say. I was an officer in the first war. The habit's in me. I'm called; I go. But that doesn't mean I'm judging you. It takes guts for a man to risk jail for his principles."

"But I have no intention of going to jail!"

"You think they'd turn you down? Is there something wrong with you? You look pretty fit to me."

"Oh, I'm fit enough. 'Food for powder,' as Falstaff says. But they can't very well jail me if I'm not in the country."

"You mean you'd go to Canada?"

"Or Sweden if Canada's not far enough."

"Oh, Mark." Seth's eyes pleaded with the misguided youth. "That wouldn't be like you. To scuttle off and dodge the issue."

This angered Mark. "You'd rather have me rot in prison?"

"Much! And you wouldn't have to rot."

"Grandpa, you're impossible! All those silly gentlemanly standards of yours went out with gold stars and Little Lord Fauntleroy."

Seth shook his head sadly. "I wonder if you really believe that. All right, let me concede that the war is unjust and rotten. Maybe even unconstitutional. I could argue that. But no matter how low things have sunk, no matter how depreciated our moral standards, this is still your country and you owe her the duty of taking a stand. You can say, 'Hell no, I won't go,' as they chant in the protest marches. But say it to the draft board. Shout it, if you like. I'll take your case. We'll be in it together, my boy."

Mark rudely brayed out some bars from a Sousa march: "Da-da, da-da-da, da-da-da!" For one shattering moment Seth felt something perilously close to dislike. Good God, was it conceivable that he *could* dislike Mark? He closed his eyes and counted to ten.

"I have friends, Grandpa, who are planning to get exempted by telling the draft board they're fags. Would you rather I did that?"

"Not unless you are one."

Mark shook his head wearily. "You really believe all that crap about honor, don't you?"

"I do."

"Oh, Grandpa, you're insatiable! First you blackmail me into living, and now you're trying to blackmail me into living your way."

"How am I blackmailing you?"

"You know you're the only person in the world I still give a damn about. However much I may reject your principles, I hate to disappoint you. And you *play* on that so!"

"I'll play every card in the pack to save you, my boy."

"Save me for what?"

"For a long and I hope a happy life."

Mark groaned. "Let's order lunch, shall we? And what about that other drink? Please. Or I'll leave you and go back to my room. I have a bottle there."

When Seth got back to New York that night and told Marjorie about their discussion, he found that she didn't agree with him that he had failed altogether to make a dent in Mark's resolution to flee the country.

"If he became that emotional, you must have pricked his conscience. And I wonder if you hadn't better stop going up there. I think you should let the boy work things out in his own way. I'm not at all sure that Angelica and Sam wouldn't rather have him in Canada than making public scenes here."

"You don't think it's a question of honor?"

"Oh, honor, fiddlesticks, Seth. That boy has been making Angelica thoroughly miserable. I wish he'd take himself and his screeching somewhere else."

"I didn't know that Angelica's skin was that thin. And I certainly didn't know that you were so solicitous of her feelings!"

"I'm not saying she's been the most wonderful mother in the world, of course not. But she's still my child, and all is forgiven when a child is in trouble."

"What trouble?"

"She's frightened, Seth! She's never encountered anything like this in her life before. Her own son shouting disgusting words at her over the telephone! And Sam's no help. He's simply written the boy off."

"Then the boy's the one who really needs our help."

"But will he take it? What help has he taken from you? To tell the truth, I have limited sympathy for Mark. Millions of human beings have had to put up with silly wars, unjust wars, wars carried on too long or too bloodily. It's history, that's all. Blithering on about it, after a certain point, doesn't help matters."

Marjorie had become browner and more gnarled with age, but her short bony figure exuded fortitude. Introducing a speaker at her club, presiding at a charity board meeting, even tending the roses in their garden at Cold Spring Harbor, she at all times seemed soberly occupied in preserving the few forms that separated men from beasts.

But she had not finished with him.

"I think there may be another reason for cutting down on your trips to Connecticut. Mark may end up by boring you. And the image you've constructed of him has become too important to you. Oh, how you always wanted a son!"

Seth turned away. Really, his wife could be the devil!

8

When an ashen Angelica, accompanied by a grim Sam, entered the hall of her parents' brownstone early one Sunday morning to inform them that Mark had fatally shot himself at dawn in his college dormitory, Seth, sitting as if paralyzed in the dining room, into which he and Marjorie had half-stumbled on receiving the news, knew that this was the reckoning, the fatal "evening up" of the score of his life. There was a kind of macabre justice in it. But how could his mind focus on anything but that young mangled body? What was he made of, anyway?

And yet there was more to bear, even more. Marjorie behaved as she had never behaved before. She seemed to have lost control of her wits.

"It's all your father's doing, Angelica! Mark would have gone to Sweden if he'd only let him. But no, Grandpa had to slam all the doors!" She turned furiously on her husband. "It was your damn sense of honor, wasn't it? Well, I hope you're glad to see where your honor has got us!"

"Shut up, Mother!" If Marjorie was behaving uncharacteristically, so was her daughter. Never had Seth seen Angelica so stern, so authoritative. "Daddy had nothing to do with it. Mark found the only way out of his troubles. His death was a relief to him. And I think it may be a relief to me. The whole thing's been so godawful."

"Oh, Angelica!" Sam Storey turned away as if the world and his wife were at last too much for him. Seth wondered if he didn't want to go down to his office.

"It is, Sam," Angelica continued in the same sombre tone. "And I believe it will be to you. In time. Mark couldn't go on living hating everything. And everybody."

Even me? Seth asked himself. Marjorie turned a bleak face to him. "Seth, forgive me."

"You may well have been right."

How right she had been was proven by a letter from Mark to his grandfather, posted the day before his suicide, which took three days to reach New York. Seth recognized the handwriting as he idly turned over the mail on the hall table and quickly stuck the letter in his pocket. He took it to his office to read and never showed it to a soul.

"Dear Grandpa: You will know when you read this that there is more than one way to 'stand up to be counted.' I agree with you that subterfuge about the draft is shabby. Who was the French noblewoman in the Terror who told her judges, with a shrug, 'Life isn't worth a lie'? I believe that. It's probably the only thing I do believe. But in taking a stand of resistance I have decided it's neater and cleaner to go all the way. I was amused by your letter about the Pater story. I knew you'd read it as soon as you got home and find that it ended on an 'up' note and write me crowingly about it. But Pater, like you, had always to be cleaning things up. Keep at it, old boy! You may even find that you can work *me* into one of your systems. I hope so, for your sake. Because I love you. I like to think there's one desperate little light flickering in the darkness. If there were a god, he'd bless you."

Seth kissed the letter and then burned it with his lighter over an ashtray. After all, it was for him alone. It was hard to believe that such misery could coexist in his soul with such exaltation. But apparently it could. And Mark had cared enough to hope that it could. Which might be almost enough for him to go on living on. So he could go right on trying to be happy, however fatuously. Why should he worry about being fatuous now? Why should he worry about anything?

They That Have Power to Hurt

1

I had dreamed that an old age in Paris would be just what suited me. Oscar Wilde wrote that good Americans go to Paris when they die; I had decided not to wait. I had sucked from the fruit of my native land all it had to offer to one even as greedy as I, and now, as a bachelor of seventy-five who had survived his dearest friends (they had all been my seniors, some by many years), I hoped to sit out a tranquil senility on the porch of a café under a chestnut tree, watching the sprucely clad Gauls go briskly by, intent, as are the truly civilized, on the immediate present, oblivious of the glories and shames of the past and certainly oblivious of a small antique American gentleman, however nattily attired, however much possessed of a certain "air," who would not have disturbed them for the world, content as he was to dwell only in his memories of an undistinguished but amusing past.

I am not being modest. Modesty has never been a virtue I admired. If I did not achieve anything great as the assistant art critic of a major New York daily, or as a contributor of urbane tales to popular magazines, or even as an easily identified minor character in a couple of important American novels, I have nonetheless written one short story which achieved something like fame and is still included in anthologies of the "best," and I recently (and fatally, as it turned out) published a little record of my friendships with some of the major artists and writers of our time which I had thought might provide our academicians with some new insights into the intellectual life of Manhattan in the years immediately following the second war. These nineteen-eighties, in which I write, have witnessed a new interest in our American artistic past (perhaps to balance the fashionable shame at our American political present), and it was this which I had hoped to tap.

I should have remained silent. My memoir enjoyed only a modest sale, but it proved manna from heaven (or hell) to the English departments of some of our major universities where the "psychobiographies" of dead writers are manufactured with total immunity from moral as well as legal retaliation. I found myself the subject of many Ph.D. theses which probed with relentless speculations into the nature of my relations with Arlina Randolph,

Dan Carmichael and Hiram Scudder, and when one of my references led to the uncovering of Arlina's letters to me (she had asked me to return them to her to be "destroyed"!) in the unsifted archives of Sulka University (today the great "discoveries" are made, not in attics but in the files and storage spaces of public institutions), there was an explosion of comment that would have led one to suppose it a cache equivalent to the Boswell papers in Malahide Castle. Arlina, the *grande dame* of American letters, the aristocratic soul supposedly faithful to an elderly spouse rendered impotent by arthritis, had, on the contrary, received her "fulfillment" at the ripe age of forty-three in an adulterous affair! Great news!

My stomach turned over as I read the fulsome extravagances of smutty-minded professors entranced at uncovering the copulations of their idol. I thought of the duc de Lauzun in Saint-Simon's memoirs, concealed under the bed of the Montespan and chuckling gleefully to himself as the springs bounced to the thrustings of the Sun King. *That* is scholarship in our day! We have seen in the fantasies of our learned friends the narrow couch of Emily Dickinson groan under the added weight of a lesbian visitor, and the aging Henry James reaching a trembling hand toward the private parts of a young male admirer. And as if to excuse itself from the charge of mere pornography, Academia insists that these postulated encounters were the source of even greater art. Is not a warmer and more human note detectable in the great Arlina's prose after Venus's belated visit? I, anyway, could not detect it. I found her most convincingly described love affair in a story written not only before *me,* but even before her marriage to "Red" Suydam (who was certainly not impotent in that early day).

But why, a stranger to these professorial raptures may ask, do I object so? Is it not something for the obscure Martin Babcock to see himself elevated to the status of a priapic muse? Should I not be grateful to supply even a phallic footnote to the history of American letters? And to know that erudite teachers now divide the fiction of Arlina Randolph into pre- and post-Babcock sperm?

Perhaps I might have succumbed to some such shameful complaisance had I been awarded any credit for my share in Arlina's "renaissance." But I have not been. Not a jot. Her so-called passion is depicted as a purely unilateral affair. If one partner was raised to the glory of a cerulean sky, the other was debased to an underworld of smoky fires glinting in the darkness. Dan Carmichael's clever but malicious drawing of a young satyr, his tiny horns just emerging from his clustered curls, with an impish leer on his deceptively angelic features as he pipes a seductive tune to a group of ludicrously swooning gods and goddesses, has been reproduced in the pages of learned periodicals and interpreted as the great artist's rendering of me and my "victims."

Oh, yes, gods as well as goddesses. Hear what that grand old ham of Yankee fiction, Hiram Scudder, had to say of me in the correspondence dug out of the dead pile of his papers at Gainsville Tech:

"I agree with you about Babcock. Few of Arlina's friends felt that he was worthy of the affection she lavished on him. It is always sad to see a person of the first order chained to one of a baser tier. Martin undeniably had charm and a kind of elfin beauty. He seemed to be trying, by a sort of osmosis, to imbibe from more gifted souls some of the talent with which he had not been endowed. But *his* soul, like his personal stature, was small; he was a busy little animal who played below the belt with both sexes and had no real concept of what went on in their minds or hearts."

Certainly not below *your* belt, horrid old man, embracing young men in homoerotic hugs and extolling their youth and vigor with your stale breath!

Well, where, anyway, do I come out of all this? With the idea, certainly, that if sex be the clue to unravelling the mystery of artistic creation (and I must assume, I suppose, that it *is* a mystery), then sex had better not be viewed through the haze of romanticism which obscures even the vision of pornographers. I can provide my own lens in the form of this memorandum which may one day be found among *my* papers in some university library that accepts *any* bequest (microfilm, after all, takes up so little space) by a graduate student looking desperately for a novel aspect in the sex life of an American writer.

2

I was born in 1912, a so-called afterthought, actually a mistake, ten years after the birth of the last of four siblings born to my parents in the first four years of their marriage, so that I was raised essentially as an only child. My father was a sturdy, hearty gentleman of shallow feelings and filed ideas. As a stock-broker on Wall Street he had managed to lose the bulk of a not inconsiderable fortune, starting even before the 1929 crash, but he would never acknowledge that it was more than a transitory piece of bad luck, and he continued to haunt his clubs, giving vent, to all who would listen, to his market theories as if he were another Bernard Baruch, and leaving the management of his brownstone and his shingle cottage in Bar Harbor, Maine, to the small income and hard-pressed imagination of his plain and feverishly resourceful wife.

I say "plain," but there was an air of undoubted nobility in Mother's long, sad, brown face and tumbled, prematurely grey hair. She took the reverses of fortune as a judgment on a frivolous society and distanced herself from those friends and relatives who had better survived the crash, as if her new poverty were a monastic garb to be worn with a dignified humility, but in semi-isolation. When I was sent on a scholarship to Saint Stephen's, a fashionable New England boarding school, and protested bitterly to Mother (Father was a mere cipher in my life) that my clothes and allowance were horridly inferior to those of my classmates, she retorted that it would build my character to endure the sneers of the "purse proud." And she made the same answer when I begged her not to scandalize the Bar Harbor summer community and cost me my invitations to the swanker children's parties by taking in boarders.

I loved Mother and wanted to help her, but I decided early that we would never recover our position by her formula, and certainly not by Father's, and I learned to grit my teeth and do things my own way. I assessed my cherubic looks and my art of pleasing, and I saw, clearly enough, that the rich dangerous world which Father fatuously thought he still belonged to, and that Mother so fiercely scorned, could, however precariously, be won. The members of the Bar Harbor Swimming Club might disdain one of my parents and dislike the other, but, after all, they had always known them, and they could be cajoled into welcoming "charming young Martin," who had such a "tough time" at home.

Mother saw that I was becoming a toady and, worse, a successful one, and she minced no words in telling me so. At last, in my passionate resistance to what I considered her smothering influence, I said things to her that she could not forgive. Ah, that was it; that was what did it! Mothers should always forgive; the gate to redemption should be ever ajar. I thought, when she at last gave me up and accepted my dedication to Mammon with a shrug of contempt, that I was relieved, but of course I wasn't. The iron had entered into my soul, and no amount of surface gaiety could ever quite cover it. I hated Mother because I loved her.

At boarding school when, at age fourteen or thereabouts, the boys had begun to lift their heads out of the dusty cellar of wanton blows and wisecracks and to see one another dimly as fellow humans, I was able to make friends with the more prominent and popular of my classmates, compensating for my lack of heftiness with amiability and wit. Teen-age boys are not accustomed to sympathy and interest from their contemporaries, and a little precocity in this field can do wonders for a social climber. I also knew how to turn a crowd against an enemy with a deadly but smilingly delivered commentary on some particularly vulnerable aspect of his personality. It is good to be sometimes feared.

My good looks were usually an important asset, but not always. They were on one occasion a decided liability. In the annual school play I was cast as the heroine with a blond wig, and so striking was my beauty and coyness of manner that two school prefects, one the captain of our football team, fell in love with me and abducted me to the cellar of the chapel, where they took turns necking with me. I will not say that this experience was the origin of a mild taste for homoerotic pleasures which has never entirely deserted me, but it certainly did not contribute to a normal development. The worst part of it was that word got out, and I achieved a reputation that followed me to Yale and was almost surely responsible for my failure to be tapped by the senior society which I had passionately coveted, the dapper and urbane Scroll & Key. Even today, when I think of this and remember our old headmaster, the holy of holies, drivelling on in his God-drunk sermons about purity and manliness while *that* had gone on beneath his pulpit, I feel a wild rage at the hysterical hypocrisy of those times.

Thus the pattern of my life was set, changing very little from college to my thirty-fifth year, when I first met Arlina Randolph. I was always well liked, even at times the "life of the party," but never the *most* popular, never truly respected by the puritanically serious, suffering a bit from the taint of the clown. In the navy, in the second war, I started as an ensign on an admiral's staff in Washington and ended there as a senior lieutenant. My imagination and diplomatic skills rendered me indispensable to the old boy, who refused to release me for sea duty, but I coaxed him to send me on safe missions to dangerous war zones and was thus able to sport all three area ribbons and even one battle star on my lapel to at least *look* like a combat veteran. But of course these never fooled a real one.

Following the war, I used my service insurance money to give me a year in Italy studying painting, after which I became a newspaper art critic covering the secondary shows (my boss took the primary), gaining an audience more through my style and wit than my insight. But the thing that made me known was the single hit of the short story I have already mentioned. It was the tale of a man who suffered from a lifelong terror that his immunity from the hideous executions of history — the hangings and quarterings, the racks, the floggings, the burnings alive — would have to be paid for in some future existence. But when he dies, he finds that he is not a victim but an executioner. He must, with full awareness of the agony he is inflicting, wield the axe, pull the cord, light the faggots. It is true hell at last.

My many friends expected great things of me after the acclaim that greeted this much reprinted tale. But it seemed I was doomed to be a "one story" man. I never hit the same note again. At thirty-five I was like the man in Mallock's *The New Republic*, of whom it was said, first, that he had a future, and later that he *might* have one, and finally that he might have had.

But that was not the whole "me." I have

not been a mere leech on the fair skin of a prosperous society. I have always wanted to give as well as take. I am too much of a true epicure not to realize that the good life involves the hand that comforts as well as that which takes. If I have practiced some harmless wiles to open doors not at first thrust wide to greet me, I have still wanted everyone in the interiors attained to be happy there. If I have had affairs with beautiful and elegant women, ever ready to smile on a pleasant unattached young man with a literary flavor, I have always ended them, I hope, with tact and kindness. I have entertained an odd little faith in my own ability — sometimes conceived almost as a duty, perhaps even as a kind of mission in (or excuse for) my life — to augment the well-being of every person with whom I found myself in any serious relationship. And never did opportunities for such augmentation more abound than in the salon of Arlina Randolph.

3

It was Dan Carmichael who introduced me to that august circle. He was then, in 1947, at age fifty, just past the peak of his great reputation as the last exponent of the Ashcan School, but if he had begun to decline, no one would have anticipated the low esteem in which his name is held today. He was a big, bony, black-haired, hirsute, oleaginous man whose angry canvases of Coney Island bathers, drunken sailors and crowded urban streets on hot summer nights had been considered appropriately powerful and radical in the Depression years. Ordinarily my editor would have reviewed his last show, but he happened to be ill, and I had the chance to write the column which pleased the great man and earned me an invitation to visit him in his studio on the top of his brownstone in Chelsea.

His ego, I found, was insatiable, but I knew how to satisfy it, and I was soon accorded the privilege of dropping in whenever I chose for a drink and a chat, of which I took full advantage, as I saw a longer and perhaps important article in it for me.

One afternoon I met him at his front door about to go out. "This is well met, young fellow! I'm off to the Suydams'. It's one of their Wednesdays. Come along. You'll like them, and I think they'll like you."

I followed him down the street in docile compliance. "Who are the Suydams?"

"I thought you knew everyone. She's Arlina Randolph."

Well, of course I knew who *that* was. Like Carmichael's, her reputation was then near its peak, but it was not, despite some rather slick later novels, to dip thereafter as low as his. The feminist movement may have sustained it a bit, but her best books, I feel sure, will bear the test of time. I had read and loved all she had written to the date of that first visit. I knew she was born in Richmond of an old Virginia family, one member of which had married a daughter of Jefferson's, and that she had been a passionate student of the Reconstruction. Her finest novels — historical ones, I suppose, as their action occurs in the decades immediately preceding her birth — deal with the travails of war-impoverished tobacco planters rebuilding their shattered world, but at the same time virtually reenslaving their blacks. More recently she had turned her lights on the current New York scene, and although her satire was keen, her prose luminous and her plots deft, these later fictions were not bathed in the nostalgia which, at least in my view, gave to their predecessors their peculiar moral beauty.

She was married, Dan informed me as we rode east in a taxi, to a rich older man, Red Suydam, now an arthritic victim confined to a wheelchair, who, although high-toned and high-handed with others, was yet content to regard himself as a privileged high priest in charge of the temple of his wife's art. He maintained her in a beautiful red brick Federal mansion in Gramercy Park, where they provided a buffet supper for a weekly salon of mixed artistic and social folk.

When Dan and I arrived, the great lady was not yet down. It was her habit to wait until most of what Proust's Madame Verdurin would have called her "faithful" had assembled. Dan led me up to where our host was sitting in his chair by the fire.

"I read your little piece on Dan's last show," Suydam informed me with snapping, malignant eyes as Dan retreated out of earshot. "He certainly must like you for *that* one."

I took a moment to assess his tone before answering. He had a long, oblong, cadaverous countenance with steely grey hair, presumably once red, and reddish eyeballs.

"You think I went too far?"

"Oh, not so far as I should have gone! I should have compared him with Michelangelo."

"Indeed? You don't think that would have flattered him?"

"I said compare, not equate, young man. Dan shares a fault if not a virtue with the Tuscan master."

"And what may that be?"

"He can't paint women. His are all brawny men with tits."

I laughed. "But his men are very male, you will admit."

"Oh, they are that! Those sailors with muscular thighs bursting their tight pants." Here the old boy winked at me. "Scrumptious, don't you think? Can you imagine them in bed with Dan's scrawny females?"

"Do you imply they go to bed with each other?"

"*I* don't. Dan does. At least in his pictures. Have you ever met Mrs. Carmichael?"

"Actually, I haven't."

"He won't be apt to introduce you. He never brings her here, poor woman. I guess she sits at home and looks at the sailors."

Another guest came up to greet him, and I was able to make my escape to look at the pictures on the high white walls. They were all American, the finest examples of Hassam, Robinson, Glackens, Sloan, Innes and, of course, Carmichael. I was too enthralled with these to bother with the other guests until I caught sight of my hostess pausing on a landing of the stairway and glancing down at the crowd.

I think I knew right away that a change had come into my life. It was not anything as banal as falling in love at first sight; it was rather the appearance in my too familiar sky of a new planet, a fine glowing orb of still undetermined influence but with an effect on the gravity of minor astral bodies that was bound to be felt. Her tall, full, firm figure, clad in blue velvet, her fine firm nose and strong chin, her alabaster skin and large pensive dark eyes gave her the air of a priestess of classic times, a Norma erect before an altar. Her hair was long and blond. I assumed it was dyed. It wasn't. Descending the stairs, she noted the staring new guest and came directly over to me.

"Who is this nice new friend?" she asked gravely as she extended her hand.

When I told her and explained my auspices, she nodded, complimented me on my "hell" story and led me to a corner, where we both sat. A maid brought her a glass of white wine.

I later learned that she was not to be interrupted by others in that corner. Her rules were simple but definite.

We talked about writing, and she treated me charmingly as an equal. I asked her why she had never written about the antebellum South, the old planters in their heyday.

"Because it was too long ago. Henry James said in one of his wonderful prefaces that the charm of the past as used in fiction depended on its proximity. It had to be almost touchable. He likened it to climbing a ladder to peer into your neighbor's garden. Some of the charm was lost if you could see a whole line of other gardens stretching into the distance. The Victorians knew that. Think how many of their novels are laid in the period of their authors' childhood or just before. *Vanity Fair*, *Middlemarch*, *Wuthering Heights*."

"And I suppose in your childhood the memory of Reconstruction was still vivid."

"And still bitter!" she exclaimed. "My grandparents were very far from reconstructed. Oh, very far! Yet there were some rare souls who saw it as a period of something like redemption. My father was one of those. He used to say that slavery was the cancer of the Old South. That a moral code with such a flaw in it must have been jerry-built. That the whole society had to be taken apart and put together anew."

Her articulation was astonishingly precise. She might almost have been reading aloud, without an *er* or an *ah*. And she seemed to have lost all trace of a Southern accent. Her tones were high and sharp, more the voice of New York than of Richmond.

"You don't mean he saw the war as a spiritual one? Like the Crusades?"

"My dear young man, he ran away from home at the age of sixteen in the last year of the war to fight for General Lee. The Yankees had nothing to do with his moral struggles. He loathed them!"

"Would you have fought for Lee had *you* been a young man then?"

"Of course I would!" Her laugh was hearty and infectious. "Do you see me as a fatuous Mrs. Howe scribbling down the inane verses of her battle hymn as she watched a review of the Army of the Potomac? No, Mr. Babcock, I would have been like our sainted general. With a heavy heart I would have shouldered a musket and gone to die for my native state!"

As she clapped her hands together, I had a vision of Boadicea, of Zenobia, of Joan of Arc. And I wondered how heavy that heart would have been. There might have been too much joy in battle.

It was time for her to join her other guests. But I had made the grade. When I left that night, she said, "Come back, Mr. Babcock. Come back to us, please."

And I did. I became the most faithful of her faithful. Arlina's salon had probably the best conversation in New York. The people who came for cocktails and supper, and stayed to talk (unless it was a musical evening) until midnight (Arlina always retired on the stroke of twelve), were a mixture of writers, journalists, painters and musicians, with a goodly number of the more enlightened members of the banking and legal communities. They talked in groups, unless a particularly burning topic united the chamber in a general discussion, moderated by Red Suydam. Otherwise, he took an almost violent interest in every subject, wheeling his chair furiously from group to group, cackling with sometimes cruel laughter, for he loved to pounce on the ridiculous, even when a half-decent compassion would have spared it.

My enthusiam for Arlina's salon did not blind me to the fact that she paid a certain price for her high sense of decorum. Because she would not tolerate drunkenness, bad language, too heated arguments or too casual dress, some of the major artists and writers of the day, including too many of the younger ones, made no appearance under her roof. She was quite aware of this herself, but she pointed out to me, with some truth, that geniuses were rarely as good talkers as near geniuses and that conversation, after all, was more the point of her gatherings than the furnishing of food and alcohol even to the sublime. I had to agree with this, but I did not go on to tell her that convention and respectability lent a faint tinge of things *passés* to her salon. Hiram Scudder, the hoary old veteran of an earlier radicalism, whose "big" novel about steel strikers in 1905 had aroused the literary world, seemed, with his hoarse croaking and false teeth, a bit of a museum piece, while Dan Carmichael's shrill denunciations of the new abstract Impressionists betrayed a senescent imagination. Time, so to speak, had dressed the old pioneers in dinner jackets.

Yet the milieu formed the perfect background for Arlina herself. She was at her best and brightest with a certain formality in the conversational give-and-take, where a witticism was never lost in a babble of conflicting voices and where a pause could signify reflection on what one's interlocutor had just said and not simply the rehearsal of one's own next *mot*. And her laugh, her wonderful laugh, could unite any group in good humor. She had the remarkable gift of making reserve seem almost intimate.

Sometimes, inevitably, to so frequent a guest as myself, her machinery showed from under its smooth cover. In spring, when she planned excursions out of the city for a select few — for a picnic on the Palisades or a visit to her Westchester "farm" — there was a slight strain in the very perfection of her arrangements and in the precision of her instructions to guests: who was to bring what or wear what or take whom. Some even breathed the word *bossy,* though it would have been kinder to say that she could never quite take in the fact that many people would rather be wrong in their own way than right in hers. The only person to whom she consistently deferred was Red. Hiram Scudder, who had known her the longest, told me that her husband, and he alone, had inherited the subservience with which she had honored her late parents.

I was soon her particular favorite. At picnics she assigned me to most tasks, and I fetched and carried for her like a faithful dog. She was certainly not one to suffer fools gladly, but once admitted to her inner circle one could relax and even indulge in an occasional bad pun. And she was a good sport, too. She could take sallies at her own expense from the initiated. Once on a country outing, where we played a word game of associations (I would say "dog," and you had to say the first word that came into your head, like "cat") and I had totalled up Arlina's responses, I announced to the group that her primary concerns appeared to be "clothes and men."

"Youth, youth," she murmured. "You are so cruel."

She took a personal interest in my life and work and did not hesitate to scold me.

"Your trouble, Martin, is that you are lazy. You should *make* yourself write. You should assign certain hours of the week to composition and stick to your program no matter what."

"Do *you* do that?"

"No, because I don't have to. I can afford to wait for the mood, because I now know that the mood will come. But when it does come I give it full sway. Even if Red and I are travelling in Europe on a fixed schedule, and I feel the mood, then I must stay where I am and write. Red is an angel about changing accommodations."

"But he's still a taskmaster. He *makes* you write."

"He doesn't make me do a thing. He simply insists that I follow my bent. I tell him we should hang a sign on our door: 'Arlina and Red, Makers of Fine Fiction.' "

What *was* their relationship? It was obvious

that it couldn't have been a physical one for several years. And before that? They had no children, which was no proof of anything, but it struck me that there was something virginal in Arlina's air. Dan Carmichael, who delighted in sexual speculations, claimed to have had it from Red himself that Arlina had been so frigid and inexperienced at the time of their wedding that it had taken him three months to consummate the marriage. But Dan's imagination was an embroidering one; I did not trust it.

The first time Arlina and I discussed the relation between the sexes was when we were seated on a bench in Bryant Park, whither we had strolled on a mild early spring afternoon following a matinée of *Tristan und Isolde.* I had been asked to fill Red's subscription seat because he hated Wagner. He had missed, however, one of the great performances of all time — Flagstad and Melchior — and Arlina, who had been deeply affected, was moved to speak of the "tragedy" of illicit love.

"Is there anything in art more shattering than the surprising of the lovers in Act Two? They have almost escaped the harsh dry world of daylight — the meanness of things too clearly delineated — into the enchantment of night — death, if you will — I don't care — and bang! Melot breaks in. Marke breaks in. All hell breaks in."

"Just before their orgasm."

Arlina paused — judicially — as if to consider whether I was being crude or merely explicit. "Well, yes, if you choose to construe the music that way."

"Isn't it unmistakable? Those rhythms?"

"I know what you mean, of course. But to me Wagner is expressing more than just that. The lovers have reached a point where their relationship is the only reality. Marke and Melot and even the warning Brangäne are irrelevancies. The terrible thing about unsanctified love — unsanctified, that is, by law or religion or mores or even by a decent regard for one's spouse or betrothed — is that these irrelevancies are always bound to intrude. Even if they're not actually intruding, they may be intruding in the lovers' minds. The lovers are never *free.*"

"But isn't that just what makes their love so great? The difficulty? Even the danger?"

"Oh, Martin, what a superficial view! How *can* you?"

"Because it's true! Look what's happening today. People everywhere are obsessed with removing the impediments to love. Easy divorce threatens the very existence of adultery. Our most respectable debutantes are permitted love affairs, and every kind of sexual perversion is freely tolerated, at least in the best society. And is anyone happier? Of course not! Because the pleasure of love is diluted with its availability. The nun in a convent who nurses a guilty passion for the priest who officiates at mass gets as much kick out of it as the busiest Don Juan on Park Avenue!"

"You can't be serious!"

"Never more so. If King Marke, stumbling on the lovers, had said, 'Go to it, kids. I only quit the hunt for a date with Brangäne,' there'd have been a terrible let-down. I bet they wouldn't have got going again until they'd quaffed the rest of that love potion."

"Don't be so disgusting." But the reproach in her voice was mild. The topic intrigued her. "It's all very well for *you* to talk that way. There are no impediments for a bachelor."

"Are there not, Arlina?" I turned to look into her eyes with an expression of mock ardor.

"Don't be silly."

And she rose to walk on.

But the sudden rigor in her tone gave me my first notion that perhaps what she minded was that the ardor was mock.

And was it? My feelings about the wonderful Arlina were mixed indeed. On the lowest level — and that was where I always started —

there was the itching yen of a small randy male for a fine large female figure, the lust of a Nibelung to pollute a Rhine maiden, or, translated into terms of literary competition, the drive of a scribbler to equate himself in the only way he could think of with a novelist of the first rank.

But that was far from the whole. By my own half-serious philosophy of love, just enunciated, I might have diluted such intensity as I was capable of in a series of easy affairs, but I still know that I was more devoted to Arlina than to any other woman in my life. She had become the warmest of friends, a kind of sisterly mentor to a man rejected by his own mother, and I cannot think of her even today without a return of something like the old heartache.

At any rate, after our Bryant Park chat, I began seriously to entertain the idea that it might be one of the delightful functions of my idle life to make some contribution to her deeper happiness.

It was Hiram Scudder who first hinted to me that my project was not entirely unfeasible. I had become a great favorite of the paunchy, bald old boy, who was always asking me to lunch, ostensibly to discuss my writing but really to hold forth about his own, and he would walk slowly down the avenue afterwards, his arm entwined with mine, while he chanted about what he would do if he had again, like me, "a manly vigor and youth." In parting he would seize my head with both his hands and plant a wet kiss, presumably of benediction, upon my forehead. Perhaps he thought of the emotion I aroused in him as paternal. Unlike Dan, who, though married, was a notorious wooer of young men, Hiram was a bachelor and very possibly a virgin to both sexes. Such things were not uncommon to his generation. Arlina's court had a decidedly androgynous note, although Red himself was given to tasteless antipederast jokes. But then Red, perhaps out of bitterness at his own incapacities, was anti everything. Except, of course, Arlina.

On one of our postprandial promenades Hiram referred to the obvious problem in Arlina's life.

"A handsome woman like that needs a different kind of love from what poor old Red can give her."

"You don't believe she's sublimated all that into something higher?" I raised my eyebrows in jest.

He chuckled. "No more than you do, young man. What she needs is a warm body two nights a week."

"What a disgusting old satyr you are,

Hiram. How do you know she hasn't got one?"

"Because I know Arlina. And I know the body she might pick if she had her choice." Here he pressed his arm closer to mine. I pulled away from him.

"Well, I know no such thing. So far as I'm concerned she's entirely devoted to her old Red. Who strikes me, by the way, as a man who might not hesitate to put a bullet through her if he caught her out. And one in her lover as well."

"You see him bursting in on them in his wheelchair? Besides, he wouldn't object. He's told me as much."

"Really?" I didn't want to encourage the old bawd, but I *was* interested.

"Oh, yes. He told me he hadn't been any good to her in that department for several years. And that he wouldn't mind if she took a lover, so long as she was discreet about it."

"And has he told her so?"

"Oh, no. That would outrage her. If it came at all, it would have to come as a passion strong enough to overcome her sense of duty. I agreed with Red. If it wasn't big enough to do that, it wasn't worth having."

I said no more on the subject, but I gave it careful thought. The removal of Red as a jealous husband certainly cleared the field. I had little zest for violence.

One Saturday afternoon when Arlina and I were walking in the fields of her Bedford farm, she suddenly put a question to me which seemed to be aimed at a very personal aspect of my own life.

"My new novel involves an adultery in Gotham which the characters must keep very secret. My heroine is a Park Avenue matron with a girl at Miss Chapin's School and a boy at Buckley. Her lover is a law partner of her husband's and is married to her own first cousin. They wouldn't go to a hotel, would they?"

"They might. A second-class one on the West Side. But she'd hate that, and if she were ever spotted on the street in that part of town, it would be fatal. No, they'd be more apt to meet in a rented apartment, still on the West Side but south of Central Park, near the shopping district, so her presence in that area, if noted, would seem natural."

"And they'd arrive and leave, of course, separately."

"Of course."

"Would she have a cleaning woman for the flat?"

"He would arrange that. The woman would never see her, and she'd leave nothing in the room that could identify her."

"And when the lovers met socially, they'd

be careful to act naturally."

"Unnaturally! The thing to avoid would be any appearance of avoiding each other. That's always a sure give-away."

"I suppose if my heroine had an unmarried lover, they could meet in his flat."

"Depending on where it is. Elevators are dangerous."

"You *do* seem to know the ins and outs."

Ah, that was what I had been waiting for! *That* had nothing to do with her novel.

"Well, you don't suppose I've been living like a monk all these years, do you?"

"Far from it."

"Would you have wished me to?"

"I?" She seemed startled. "Why, no, I don't suppose I should. What right have I to be your censor?"

"The right I freely give you. The right of a friend I love and respect above all others."

"But, dear Martin, your private life is your own affair!"

"Not anymore. Now that my life is under discussion, I want you to know I've been pure as Hippolytus since the day we met."

We had been walking by the stile that separated the field from her neighbor's. She turned now to lean against it, facing me, but with clenched fists raised to her eyes.

"What are you trying to tell me, Martin?"

"It's pretty obvious, isn't it?"

"Oh, dear friend, please don't play games with me. I'm not up to that kind of thing."

"It isn't playing games to be in love with you."

"Love!" She dropped her hands, and I saw something like terror in her eyes. "You can't love me. You're a mere boy compared to me. A dear, beautiful boy who should be loving some dear, beautiful girl. Do you want to drive me out of my mind? *Do* you?"

"That's just what I want to do." I stepped forward and seized both her hands in mine. I stared at her averted eyes until they turned to me. "There are eight years between us, which is nothing at our ages. Let *me* decide about that 'dear, beautiful girl.' The only woman I want is *you,* and I'm not too humble to claim we can give each other something that's better than anything either of us ever had."

Her eyes now wandered in what seemed an almost childlike confusion. "What about my husband?"

"He needn't ever know a thing. Leave all that to me. If I can do it for your novel, I can do it for you." I allowed a grave pause. "Let me kiss you, Arlina." When she said nothing, I repeated the request. "I don't want you to think I ever grabbed anything you didn't freely accord."

"Very well. Kiss me, Martin."

Whereupon I did so. Her response was all I could have wished. When we got back to the house, Hiram Scudder leered at me disgustingly. He too had been walking, and I supposed he had espied us.

4

When Arlina surrendered to love, it was without reservation. She came to my little apartment in the Village quite openly, disdaining the maneuvers of her fictional characters, on certain weekday afternoons, and we had rapturous times together. At first. But I could not quite accustom myself to the almost reverential aftermaths to our lovemaking of which she made much point. She insisted that we read aloud famous love poems to each other. As she was planning to publish an anthology of these, I could not but note that the time was not, at least in her case, entirely wasted.

I sound like a cad, but what man wouldn't who told the whole truth? The fact was that Arlina's lovemaking, at first delicious, as she shyly and then rapidly more boldly accustomed herself to every intimacy, began at last to be the least bit smothering. She was too articulately romantic, too anxious to possess every aspect of my nature. She wanted me to agree on certain times of the day or night, when we were not together, when we would think passionately of each other. She wanted to penetrate into every chapter of my past, to learn about my old love affairs, to question me about the exact quality of my feeling for her, reaching rather too greedily, it seemed to me, for the smallest evidence that she represented a unique experience in my emotional life.

I had to fabricate almost all my responses. She would have been horrified by the truth. I was only too sure that the fantasies in which all lovers indulge to keep their libidos keen were very different in our two cases. Whereas she may have made love to the remembered rhythms of *Tristan*, I enhanced my lust with images of a proud Roman dame submitting helplessly to the rape of a barbarian, her aroused appetite actually whetted by humiliation and shame. At other times I likened myself to the villain Maskwell in Congreve's *Double Dealer*, boasting how he "had wantoned in the rich circle" of Lady Touchwood's love. That was more my inner style.

It was therefore not without a feeling of a needed recess that I greeted the news that Arlina was departing with Red on a two months' lecture tour across the country to promote her new book. She was very emotional about our separation and made me promise to write her daily to the care of her trusted female agent, who would be travelling with her. I was only intermittently faithful to the task, but the many florid epistles that she indited to me were the ones that turned up in the "cache" at Sulka U.

In her absence I dropped in more often on Dan Carmichael in his studio. If I was not averse to being freed for a while from Arlina's sometimes fatiguing attentions, I missed almost at once the reassuring glow of her approbation, which had given me a novel but gratifying sense of success in life. I knew that I had aroused strong feelings in Dan, and should have left him alone, but there you have me. My nature craved this new incense of admiration from the great.

His studio was reached by a back stairway descending to the service entrance, so I did not have to encounter his bleak and saturnine spouse, who, in Red Suydam's mocking description, brooded about male models in the floor above discarding their raiment least of all to be sketched. I found Dan in a depressed mood; he complained that he could neither paint nor draw, and wanted only to talk and drink.

He did, however, one afternoon a sketch of me, executed with remarkable speed. It was a very fine likeness, and I flushed with pleasure when he said I could have it.

"But it's too valuable for a gift," I protested, more to please him than to offer it back.

"I can give what I like to my friends," he growled. "Only promise me one thing. Don't give it to Arlina."

"Why should I do that?"

"Oh, some silly notion of how a lover should behave."

"So you know about me and Arlina."

"Everybody knows about you and Arlina."

"Even Red?"

"Oh, Red indeed. He's positively obscene about you being the smaller. He says you have to sling a bucket over her head and hang on to the handle for dear life."

I was horribly mortified, but it was not my habit to show it. There had to be other ways of getting back at Arlina's sneering court.

"You say you can't draw these days." I rolled up my sketch and put a rubber band around it. I wanted to be sure to take it away with me before he changed his mind, of which he was all too capable. "But this," I added, holding it up, "is surely no example of artist's cramp."

He viewed me obliquely. "Maybe you're my only inspiration now."

My stare was cool. Had I really aroused a major passion? If so, I felt little sympathy. I needed to pay him off for the bucket crack. As I turned to go, I asked, "Is there anything I can do for *you* in return for my handsome present?"

He looked up at once. "Yes! Pose for me in the nude."

I laughed. "Dan, you old lecher. You know I'm too modest for that."

"You goddamn little prick teaser!" he exploded. "You're afraid if you stripped you might give yourself away. You're not half as straight as you like to make out. Oh, I've heard about you. Now get your hot little ass out of here!"

I laughed, with genuine good nature, and departed, taking my sketch.

But I returned only three days later, behaving as if nothing had happened. At this poor Dan broke down completely. He pleaded with me desperately to respond to his love; he blabbered about his obsession with me; he even wept as he threatened me with being the cause of the extinction of his art. It was appalling to see a great man reduced to such a state of uncontrol.

Now what was I up to? Was I still smarting about Red's cruel image of me and Arlina? Did I suspect that it was really Dan's invention and not Red's at all? A little, perhaps. But couldn't there be an understandable pride in seeing an artist of the first order (at least so he was still considered by many) grovel before you? And tell you that it was in *your* power and yours alone to enable him to pick up his brush?

Yes, but that was not all. There was still the idea of my pleasant little function in life to give some pleasure where I had received so much. And I had owed in the past year most of my pleasure to the circle to which he had introduced me.

Anyway, I did not keep Dan long on tenterhooks. I accorded him what he wanted, to my very mild and to his too furious satisfaction. Indeed, so ecstatic did he wax that, had I desired it, he would have kicked his poor old wife out of the house and established me in her stead. But of course I wanted no such thing, nor had I the least intention of continuing the liaison after Arlina's return.

Arlina's return, however, was to result in the end of both affairs. I had agreed now to pose for Dan as he had requested, and in doing so I had actually expected to be the subject of the greatest painting of his career, a nude portrait imbued with all the feeling that Dan poured into the love which, at least in his younger days, had not dared to reveal its nomenclature. But one afternoon, while I was posing, the back doorbell rang, and Dan pressed the buzzer to open it, expecting a delivery which could be left downstairs. Instead, two minutes later, Hiram Scudder pushed open the studio door without knocking and walked in.

The mistake I made was to grab a shirt and cover myself. Hiram's beady eyes leered at me; his tone was malignant.

"Oh, go on, please, go on. Let me not interrupt so charming a séance. Or are such beauties to be revealed only to the artist?"

Of course I should have brazened it out, as if it had been a routine posing, and allowed the jealous Hiram's lecherous eyes to feast on my bodily parts as we all three casually chatted. Instead, I protested that the session was over anyway and that I was already late for an appointment. Dressing hastily behind a screen, I took my leave.

Five days later I received this epistle from Arlina:

"I have had a revolting letter from hateful Hiram which has made it impossible for me to continue my tour. I have told Red that I am suffering from migraines and cannot speak in public. And so indeed I am. I cannot find it in my heart to believe it of you, dearest, dearest Martin, though Hiram says that Dan actually boasted to him of his 'conquest.' I shall, of course, hear what you have to say. I will come to you on the afternoon of the 25th. My plane gets in that morning. Oh, God, God! Have I been a fool?"

5

Arlina stood before me in my small living room whose only first-rate objects of art were the three Whistler etchings of Venice which she had given me. She was very pale and sad and grave. I remembered my initial impression of her as a pagan priestess. I had not attempted to deny or even to palliate Scudder's charge.

"You tell me it meant nothing to you. I cannot imagine a human being to whom such things mean nothing. Certainly not one with whom I have been so intimate. A man I loved!" At this she gave a little cry. "Oh, Martin, how *could* you? The moment I was gone! Did I mean nothing to you?"

"You know that's not true."

"How can I know?"

"Don't you feel it? In the deepest part of you?"

"No!"

"Then how can I help you?"

"You can't! Oh, I must face this alone. I see that." She clasped her hands and shook them in her distress. "There's no use talking. You're simply not the man I took you for. That's not your fault. There's no reason you should have been. You never claimed to be. It was my folly to erect a pedestal and put you up on it. It would have been better for me if we'd never met."

"Oh, don't say that. We had good times."

"Maybe *you* did. In your own way. Mine were illusions."

"Isn't love an illusion?"

"Ah, no cheap platitudes, please."

"Look, Arlina. Give this time to heal. You say I wasn't the man you thought me. But the man I am isn't so bad a guy. Get to know him. He and you might still be friends."

"So that's it." She shook her head sadly. "Friendship. It's your *métier,* isn't it? I suppose it's all very well. *If* you've never known the other thing."

And with this she left me.

But we did in time become friends again,

mild friends perhaps, but still friends, and we remained such until the day she died.

And now let me put the question. Did I do her any real harm? If, as the critics claim, the affair deepened her insight into the passions that "consume mankind," was she not the gainer and I a significant contributor to American letters? What did her suffering, or even Dan's, amount to? Weren't they both still on top of their worlds?

But the truth is that I had nothing to do with the nourishment of their art. Passion in great artists is as much the product of their imagination as it is of their hearts. As a skilled paleontologist can reconstruct the skeleton of a dinosaur from a single bone in its toe, so could Arlina resurrect the love of Antony and Cleopatra from the mere memory of our poor fling of an affair. Nor, if the truth be told, did she need even that. Jane Austen could create Elizabeth and Darcy, and Emily Brontë, Heathcliffe and Cathy, out of daydreams while strolling in a garden or a moor.

And so they go, the great Arlinas, supreme in the delights and consolations of their celestial visions, deriving occasional niblets of nutriment from the lesser humans on whom they occasionally feed, yet receiving the lachrymose sympathy of academic researchers for every supposed pang of "disprized love" they may incur, which love is actually only further grist for their busy mills. While as for the poor partner of this "love," well, out upon him! Who was he to play gross tunes upon the heartstrings of genius?

With scrupulous fairness, however, I append the lines which Arlina had underlined in the morocco-bound copy of Shakespeare's sonnets which she gave me one Christmas:

They that have power to hurt and will do none,
That do not do the thing they most do show,
Who, moving others, are themselves as stone,
Unmoved, cold and to temptation slow;
They rightly do inherit heaven's graces
And husband nature's riches from expense;
They are the lords and owners of their faces,
Others but stewards of their excellence.

But you know what the sestet tells of these lords and owners. They are also lilies which, when festering, smell far worse than weeds!

Trust the artist to have the last word.

The Lotos Eaters

1

Dick Emmons, in reviewing his life at seventy, thought he could justly say that the good things in it had come from his own exertions and the bad from his own bad luck. An exception might be made for his good looks, which had certainly not been of his own making, but which had contributed both to his success in the law and to the misery of his first marriage. And they continued, even at his present age, to add to his popularity in the posh little isle of his retirement, Maregrande in Florida. For how many men of seven decades were still possessed of thick wavy blond hair, only just sprinkled with grey, retreating in a triangle from a wide, lineless forehead, a firm straight nose and what his lovely second wife liked to call his "silver-grey bedroom eyes"?

His looks, however, had been his only inherited fortune, for he deemed his brain an asset he had formed himself. His parents had been the caretakers of a great country estate outside Philadelphia, the benevolent master of which had assisted their smart and handsome only child to get through college and law school at the University of Pennsylvania. Belonging to no particular social group, raised in a limbo between the old rich and the lower middle class, Dick had absorbed the discreet manners of the former by a kind of osmosis. He had almost unconsciously used the tools of his natural reserve, his orderly conduct, his neatness of appearance and his air of quiet self-confidence to gain admission to circles which did not suspect that he lacked the tickets of birth and background. The people he met seemed never to ask what his origin might have been; he was simply Dick Emmons; he always fitted in.

Graduating from law school, where he had been an editor of the review, he was immediately hired by a great New York law firm of which he became a partner after nine years of hard but interesting toil. Fortune seemed constantly to smile at him, but only that side of fortune over which he could exercise some control.

The other side was less benign. His father had been caught selling valuable furnishings of the mansion, finally unoccupied by its now senile owner; he was prosecuted by the latter's nephew and died in jail. His mother had suffered from a long, lingering and expensive terminal ailment for which, of course, Dick had to pay. After her death he had married a beautiful society girl whose psychic disability had been concealed by parents whose hope was that a happy marriage might cure it. Her manic and unfounded jealousy had caused her to make an attempt on Dick's life, following which she had taken her own. Their only child, a daughter, was retarded and had been institutionalized. It was true that many ladies had longed to console him, but for years he remained a stoical and solitary figure, scrupulous about attending the social gatherings of partners and clients, popular, even charming in his muted way, but known as a man of few pleasures and no intimates. If he had love affairs, they were very discreet ones.

Everyone, therefore, was much surprised, even shocked, when he had suddenly retired, at sixty-nine, and married a wealthy and very social widow, only a few years his junior. Joyce Klein had been a Philadelphian like himself, but of a very different milieu. She had been born a Miss Stewart, related to Drexels and Biddles, though not rich like many of those, and she had righted her economic position by marrying a much older, self-made, soft-drink tycoon. He had left her his whole estate outright, a good chunk of which she managed to retain after the bitter undue-influence lawsuit brought by the outraged offspring of his first marriage was settled. Joyce was one of those tall, skinny, dark-haired and dark-complexioned women of jerky but self-assured movements who know how to wear stylish clothes in such a way as to make both the attire and the woman seem ravishing. She was tough-minded, amusing and not unkind, and she believed that she was entitled to anything in the world that she set her mind on.

The marriage took place barely a month after their first meeting. Dick had gone to Maregrande for a week of sun and golf, staying at the beach club, where he was put up by one of his partners. There he met Mrs. Klein, who, after one long, frankly appraising glance, had invited him to dinner at her beautiful cream-colored Palladian villa by the sea. She had placed him at her right at table, talked almost to no one else, and virtually commanded him to stay on when the other guests were leaving. They had then spent a voluptuous night together.

In the morning over breakfast on the terrace, not in the least abashed by the efficient presence of her black butler, Joyce expressed her candid satisfaction with the events of the previous evening.

"It's so rare to find a contemporary who can make love like that. And I never could abide the idea of having to make up to younger men, or — perish the thought — paying a gigolo. After we met at the club yesterday I called Joe Gerwain, the old faggot who considers himself the *arbiter elegantiarum* of this isle, and he filled me in about you. I don't see why you mightn't be the answer to a rich widow's prayers. *Are* you?"

Dick was enough of a court lawyer to be able to adapt himself instantly to any new line of questioning. "Do you play golf?" he asked.

"Surely not as well as you. But on a good day I can score under ninety. Do *you* play bridge?"

"Surely not as well as you. But I like the game. I could take lessons."

"And we have no children," she mused. "Except that daughter you had to put away, and she doesn't count. And of course no parents. Really, no excess baggage at all that I can make out. Would you mind living here in Maregrande? For the winter, anyway?"

"Why, I think it's paradise! I have an apartment in New York that I'd want to keep, but that's no problem."

"None at all. I have one too. Then we might consider a match. Why don't you move your things over from the club? We'll give it a try for a couple of weeks and see how it works out."

It had worked out very well indeed. Their only quarrel occurred when she too sharply criticized, coming home from a party, how he had failed to raise one of her bridge bids, and she actually apologized when she saw his face darken. "I'm not going to jeopardize what we have for any silly card game," she concluded. They went out together to almost every house in that small community, and her friends were universally enthusiastic about him. Some were too enthusiastic.

"Don't let Elsie Kelley get too cozy with you," she warned him. "She's a hungry, designing bitch."

"Isn't Bob enough for her?"

"Hasn't she told you? She's told everyone else. Poor old Bob's been impotent since his prostate operation. She'd have no objection to sharing you with me. But I warn you. I'm jealous as a cat."

He glanced at her curiously. They were walking down the beach on a windy morning, and her blown hair partly concealed her features. It was the first time that she had alluded to any inner feeling she might have for him.

"Could this be the first symptom of a tenderer emotion?" But he immediately regretted the question, even though his tone had been jocular.

"You mean love? I've never much associated that term with myself. All I know is that when I want something, I want it to be entirely my own."

"I'm just like you."

"Are you?" Her tone implied a genuine curiosity. But how much did she care? She didn't, at any rate, wait for his answer. "I always suspect men of wanting to be moony. I should have thought your marriage might have cured you of that, but one can never be sure."

She would be taken on her own terms and none other — that was clear. If he married her, he would be marrying a stranger, but wasn't that always the case? And what, anyway, did he have to lose?

A year later he was happy to acknowledge that not only had he lost nothing; he had gained everything he dreamed of when he retired from the law. And he decided that he now owed it to Joyce, despite her dislike of what she called "mush and rot," to tell her so. He was strolling down the beach alone on a halcyon morning, watching the gulls circle and the pelicans dive and the fishing boats lie motionless far out to sea, and he returned to the house, entering the living room by a French window to find Joyce on the sofa, reading *Vogue*.

She might have been a handsome illustration herself of that magazine, dressed in blue and white against the deep blue of the rug and the white of the furniture and the huge Audubon shore birds on the walls, which brought the sea into the room.

"You know what this house, this whole island, is?" he began. "It's heaven, pure and simple."

"Heaven on earth," she corrected him, her eyes still on her page.

"Where else would heaven be?"

She glanced up now, faintly quizzical. "Wouldn't heaven be in the sky?"

"When we die?"

"Isn't that the idea?"

"Whose idea?"

"Why, most people's, I suppose. Most Christians, anyway."

"Is it *yours?*"

She frowned faintly. "What are you getting at, Dick?"

"I'm asking if you really believe that when you die you'll go to heaven."

"Are you implying that I may deserve the other place?"

"No, no, of course not. All I'm trying to find out is whether you believe in an afterlife."

Surprised, but willing to humor him, she paused to consider this. "I've never thought much about it. But yes, I suppose I do. It seems rather pointless if what we have here is all, don't you think?"

"My thinking it's pointless doesn't prove it isn't."

"Then you *don't* believe in an afterlife? You think we just go out, like a light bulb?"

"That's right. I can't imagine why any god would wish to extend the lives of billions of human grubs forever."

Joyce now firmly closed her magazine. "May I ask what you *do* believe in?"

"Certainly. That this life is all we're given. For us to make our own heaven or hell in. I've had my share of hell, though I didn't make it. It was made for me. But I resolved that I was going to have my heaven, too, when I had done my work and made my money and given such help to charities as a man of my means should. *Then* and only then would I be entitled to harps and golden streets and hosannas. Except I chose Maregrande instead."

"So *this* is heaven?"

"Why not? Everything is clean and glowing. The weather is divine. The police protect us from intruders, and the high cost of living excludes the poor. Even the ill and dying tend to remove themselves. There is no filth, no want, no bad manners, nor even any bad taste, except perhaps for your friend Elsie Kelley's

Moorish palazzo. Why should I worry about being privileged? Haven't I earned it?"

"But I wonder if *I've* earned it. I had no idea you were such a philosopher."

"Well, we haven't been married very long."

"That's perfectly true." Joyce's expression was now a thoughtful one. She rose and walked to the window. He had evoked a mood in her which was not familiar to him, and he had a chilly apprehension that he might not have done well. "We each decided that the other had, at least on the surface, just the qualities each needed, and that we didn't have to look deeper." Her back was still to him, but more intensely so as she went on. "We liked each other's bodies. Neither of us, after all, had given up in *that* department. And we had good tempers, so long, anyway, as things were going our way, and we had every reason to believe that they would keep on doing just that. We played the same games, and we both enjoyed dressing up and looking our best and partying with people whose chatter seemed less banal after a couple of cocktails."

"So what's wrong with that?" he asked, after a pause.

"Just this." She turned to him now, and her eyes were accusing. "I thought we were going to live in the same place. But we don't. You're in heaven!"

2

Brenda Carstairs, Joyce's niece, was paying an annual visit to her aunt in Maregrande. She was a big, lanky, sandy-haired, outdoorsy Philadelphia matron of some forty years, who, like Joyce, wanted to have everything her own way at home, but was warned by her perennially unemployed husband to mind her *p*'s and *q*'s when visiting the aunt on whose generosity they depended for half their income and whose last will and testament would decide the future of their children. Joyce was very free with her donations to all her siblings and was perfectly willing to underwrite the education of their offspring, but she expected in return an appropriate gratitude and the display of agreeable good manners. One great-niece had been cut off altogether for her rudeness to "Auntie" over the Viet Nam War, and a nephew who failed to acknowledge a Christmas check had had to wait three years for another. "You can think what you want and do what you want," she told her family. "I don't give a damn about your principles.

But when it comes to taking money, you've got to learn how to deal with power. *I* did."

She let Dick go off alone to the golf course that morning; she wanted to have a frank talk with Brenda. After breakfast they took their coffee cups to sit by the swimming pool.

"I've been reviewing the facts of my life," Joyce began, "and I've been wondering if I haven't been giving myself rather too good marks. It occurs to me that people down here and in New York and even in dear old Philadelphia may have a very different idea of me from the one I have of myself. For all I know, they may even despise me."

"Oh, Auntie, no!"

"Oh, Auntie, yes. Money is a great bar to intimacy. Even quite rich people are capable of kissing the asses of those who are richer. And that is why I'm appealing to you. I believe you know more people who know me than anyone else in the family. I want to hear all the horrors that are said about me. Even if they're entirely untrue. I need to know this for a plan I have of altering my life in some respects."

"But, Auntie, people admire you! They admire you immensely."

"Bullshit. Oh, some may, I grant you. But I want to test the opposition. I want to hear the gossip, all the juiciest morsels."

"But how would I know them? People wouldn't tell *me.*"

"Oh, yes, they would! A niece is just whom they'd tell. Come on now. I'll be grateful. I'll buy you that jade and gold necklace you were eyeing in the beach club store."

Brenda's temptation was almost comically obvious. "Oh, Auntie, I couldn't!"

"You mean it's so bad?"

"Well, you know how vicious some people can be. Particularly when they envy you."

Joyce took in her niece's continued hesitation with a sardonic smile. "Of course, I know you're dying to tell me. Few can resist the pleasure of saying something disagreeable, even to their nearest and dearest. But you're afraid that when this morbid mood of mine shall have passed, I'll resent the things you've told me. Now be fair, Brenda. Even if you think I'm hard as nails, you must admit I'm as good as my word. Well, then, I give you my word I shan't hold it against you. In fact it's the other way round. I'll be mad as hell if you *don't* tell me."

"Very well, Auntie. Let's start with Maregrande." Brenda, reassured now, paused, as before a tray of sweet savories. "One thing they say is that you wheedled Mr. Klein out of his entire estate when he was senile and dying."

"Well, I knew that his children hated me. I knew that I'd have to settle with them. But I wanted to be in the driver's seat, and I was. They got plenty."

"But they had to sue for it."

"Otherwise I'd have had to. I don't suppose anyone tells you that Lucas Klein hated them, and with every justification. I don't suppose anyone gives me the credit for being the only person in the world who ever made the old geezer happy."

"Oh, Auntie, *I* know that. But do you expect the world to be charitable?"

"Any more than I am? No. Go on."

"They say your creed is that all the world's for sale. To the highest bidder."

"And it's not?"

"And they say you bought Dick."

"That, of course, is nonsense. He's much too well off. But that'll do for this kindly island. What do *your* friends, your contemporaries, think of me?"

"Well, careers are the great thing with them now. With the women, anyway. They think you should have had a job of some sort."

"Even if I employ women? How many in this house alone?"

"Oh, servants don't count. They say you're nice to your servants the way you're nice to your dogs."

Joyce reflected that this last was probably Brenda's own contribution and reminded herself of her pledge of exoneration. "So I should have been a lawyer or a banker, is that it? But mightn't I have found myself working on some other woman's taxes or portfolio? Miss Ingris in the Cravath firm must spend hours on my capital loss carry-overs alone. Isn't it enough to keep other women busy without taking from them the things they're busy over?"

"They don't seem to see it that way."

"Well, skip them. What do my old Philadelphia pals say about me?"

"Oh, they're more moralistic. They say you're a drone. That you don't even occupy yourself with any good works."

"And what, pray, is a good work? Is it nothing to play the best game of bridge on this island? And to have built the handsomest house? And to wear the prettiest clothes? What is life if nobody sets a style? What is a capitalist state if nobody shows the rich what they can do with their riches? Must everyone work in a soup kitchen or a settlement house? There has to be elegance, damn it all! There has to be some beauty in life!"

"Auntie, please remember it's not I who say these things!"

"Oh, I know. You've been a good girl, and

you shall have that necklace. But I do get mad when I hear people yammering about doing charitable work. Have they tried? Don't they know it's all done by professionals these days? Go to any hospital, any school, any museum. It's not your helping hand they want, thank you very much; it's your hard cash. And I give it to them, pots of it. I don't think you'll find me bad-mouthed by many of the major charities in New York City. What else do people suggest I should be doing with my life?"

"There are always causes, I suppose. My children talk about doing things for civil liberties."

"You mean protests? Marches? Stopping traffic and shrieking obscenities? All they accomplished was to elect Reagan."

"Well, then, Auntie, you're right. There's nothing left."

"Oh, but there is, dear, there is." Joyce nodded her head gloomily. "How could I not know? Fund raising is left. One of the main reasons I came down here was to get away from it. But how can one? It has swept our world. We dance for cancer; we dine for art; we drink for education. The widow's mite is only a come-on for the foundation grant."

"Well, there you are, Auntie. Everyone admits you were the ultimate fund raiser. The acknowledged queen of the charitable ball!"

"Heavens! A compliment at last."

"I remember when you raised half a million dollars for Saint Bartholomew's Hospital at a single party! It was fancy dress, and you were photographed in *Life* as . . . was it a storm cloud?"

"I was the Spirit of Niagara." Joyce allowed herself a little quiver of pride. "It's nice of you to remember. I *did* do it rather well, if I say so myself. And I daresay I could do it again. I'm always being asked. Just the other day they wanted me to do a ball for the opera. I said no, but it may not be too late to change my mind."

"But why should you want to do that when you love it so down here?"

"Why?" Joyce laughed in sudden amusement. "Why, to earn my ticket to heaven, that's why!"

3

Dick offered to go with Joyce when she told him that she had accepted the chairmanship of the opera ball, but she briskly informed him that she would much prefer to have him stay in Maregrande.

"What would you do in New York? I'll be on the telephone all day long, out to lunch, giving cocktail parties to organize committees, and God knows what else. You'd be bored stiff and in my hair. The good Lord only left *his* heaven to create a new world, and this will be a rather bad old one. In fact, a paradise lost."

"But I can't help wondering if I'll ever get you back. You've been behaving so oddly of late."

"How oddly?"

"I don't really know."

"Then it can't have been too odd. But I'll promise you this, dear. If I don't come back, you can come to me. Does that make it better?"

"I suppose so" was his sulky response.

When she had gone, smiling back at him with a rather fixed cheerfulness as she passed quickly through the security gate, he felt unaccountably abandoned. Who and what *was* this remarkable creature he had married? Did she love him at all? Did she love anybody? Had she ever? Why, if she was coming back, or if she would allow him to join her if she didn't, did he feel so desolate?

The weeks that followed only deepened his sense of depression. Joyce telephoned every other day at six P.M. in the same perfunctorily cheerful mood. Was he playing golf and who with? Was he going out for dinner? How was the weather? Yes, she was very busy. And yes, thanks, the party sales were going well. She even hoped to make another record. But his feeling that she was in another world, perhaps for good, continued to unsettle him.

Maregrande without her seemed to lose much of its charm. It was not, certainly, that the little community failed to look after him; he had a golf foursome every morning and a dinner party every night. But he was now more sharply aware of the daily complaints of his male friends; in the club bar after his game they were constantly deploring the faults of the world from which they had withdrawn: its political extremism, both right and left, its sexual permissiveness, its scorn of ideals and standards, its drugs and crime. Why, if they had got away from all that, did they harp on it so? Because they had left descendants as hostages? But often enough they deplored these descendants as well. The ladies at dinner were better — more lively, anyway — but they displayed an almost morbid interest in the smallest details of their neighbors' lives. It was not just gossip, either; a new garden plot, the redecoration of a living room, a throat infection, commanded almost the same attention as a double adultery. Did that mean they were more alive than the men, who cared, so far as the island was concerned, only for themselves? He wasn't sure.

Elsie Kelley took prompt advantage of Joyce's absence to suggest her standard cure for his loneliness.

"I could come over any evening at six. Bob takes a nap at that time, and anyway, he doesn't give a damn."

"Are you suggesting that I *tromper* my wife in her own bed?"

"Do you think I don't know every house on this island? Joyce has three guest rooms, not counting the pool house."

"And you call yourself her friend!"

"I don't call myself anything, honey boy. You're the man with the labels."

"I don't think you'd like the one I have for you."

Elsie was furious; that was not the way a gentleman of her world turned down what he should at least have regarded as a flattering invitation. She proceeded to invent horrid stories about him and spread them all over the island, but although these were eagerly listened to, and even sometimes repeated to him, his inviolable status as an extra man spared him from any form of social interdict. To fill an empty seat at a dinner or card table the hostesses of Maregrande would have made do with a serial killer.

At one dinner party he was relieved to find himself the neighbor of Joyce's most likeable friend, Eugenia Hoyt, the "intellectual" of the community, a genial, pleasant and widely read woman who had cheerfully adapted herself to the company of the unreading. When he confessed to her his waxing disillusionment with the island, she asked him, "You find us too sanitized?"

"Perhaps that's it. I find myself yearning for all the nasty urban blights I was so happy to get away from: the crowding, the pushing, the rudeness. Even the homeless."

"But not the crime, I hope?"

"No, I don't suppose I actually want to be mugged. But I resent the immense precautions we take down here to be sure we're not."

She nodded in partial sympathy. But only partial. "You think we've lost touch with reality. I know the feeling. But of course Maregrande is just as real as Manhattan. And people have a right, I suppose, if they can afford it, to purchase their own brand of reality. What I think is important to realize is that most of them get what they want. For make no mistake they *love* Maregrande just as it is. They aren't jaded or bored. They're *happy,* Dick. And happiness is such a rare quality on this planet that I have learned not to sneeze at any who have achieved it."

"I see. *I'm* the one who's out of step. I don't say that the people here are any worse than people anywhere else. It may be simply that the very prettiness of the life here makes their less pretty qualities stand out more."

"What's wrong with you, my friend, is what's wrong with me. We miss our Joyce. Do you remember how in Wagner's *Rheingold*, when the giants abduct Freia, the gods grow old without the rejuvenation of her golden apples? Bring back our Freia, Dick! Please!"

He thought of this conversation a week later when he read in the *Times* of Joyce's triumph with her opera ball. The climax of the party had occurred, the reporter noted, when Mrs. Emmons, receiving the guests at the top of the stairway of the Plaza Ballroom, had greeted the sensational new Brünnhilde of *Die Walküre* with a ringing "Hojotoho!"

He called her that night to congratulate her, but she cut through his effusion.

"How's heaven?"

"Hellish."

"You miss me?"

"Abominably."

"I like that."

"Then you must be a masochist. Will you come back now?"

"That depends. On whether or not you've learned your lesson."

"You mean that I love you? Oh, but I have. I do!"

"Good God! Have you been up to something with Elsie Kelley? Only a guilty man could be so banal."

"I *loathe* Elsie Kelley."

"You say that as if you meant it. Good. No, your lesson was to learn that you had not achieved heaven on your own merits. That *I* was your heaven. And that I could jolly well take it away whenever I chose."

"That lesson has been learned. But you certainly sound very superior tonight. Had you no lessons to learn yourself?"

"Oh, yes. One. I wanted to see if I had to earn *my* heaven. By works, it would have to be, for I find now that I have little faith. By loving my neighbor as myself, wouldn't that be the way? But I found I loved myself too much. Then I thought it might be enough if I made a heaven for *you*."

"But wouldn't it have to be reciprocal? Wouldn't we each have to make the other's heaven? And I don't kid myself that I can make yours."

Her pause seemed to concede that this might be the case. "Well, if it's *more* blessed to give than to receive, doesn't that suggest that there may be *some* blessedness in receiving?"

He laughed. "So we can both be saved. Fine. Come home, sweetie!"

"I told you not to call me that! But if you promise never to do so again, I think I will come back. I don't see why we shouldn't be adequately happy in Maregrande. At least until you have your first stroke. And even then, with any luck, you may still be able to play bridge."

"And how about you?"

"Oh, you know I'll hit a hundred. In perfect health. I'm just the type."

He smiled as she rang off. He was only too sure she was.

The Renwick Steles

When Osborne Renwick attained his sixty-second birthday, in the dark depressed winter of 1933, he had been married exactly half his life. But it seemed to him that his union with the "incomparable" (as she was apt to be termed) Sophonisbe, a decade his junior, had embraced a much larger portion of his existence, as they were also first cousins, and their families had lived in adjoining brownstone cubes on lower Fifth Avenue. Her father and his, brothers and members of an old Manhattan real estate concern, had each sired an only child. Sophonisbe's, the elder and senior partner, had left her a fortune which still, even in the low market of that day, was worth a dozen millions; his own had left him an amount something less than a quarter of that sum. Had he married anyone else, he would have been considered a rich man.

But he had not married anyone else. He had married a famous woman, or one who, soon enough after their match, had made herself one. The great rambling Tudor mansion in

Greenwich, which she had modeled after one in Sussex where Queen Elizabeth (Sophonisbe's ideal of a woman) had been wont to visit, was featured in every picture book of famed American houses, and the many acres about it had been cultivated into a spectacular arboretum which her will would one day devise to the State of Connecticut to be managed by the same trustees who presided over the museum in Hartford which she had created and filled with American arts and crafts. Osborne, who in contrast to his consort's seeming impregnability to time, had waxed white and soft and stout with the years, felt like a retired but well-pensioned and cosseted staff member when, seated with a book of poetry in the solitude of a garden bench, he heard the approach of Sophonisbe's high, bell-like tones as she conducted a tour of botany students down the paths, and he would flee to the security of the maze to hide himself in the beauty of a "green shade." But he would wonder at such moments if there might not have been an excess of beauty in his life.

It was not that Sophonisbe forced anything on him. If she had the ability, she had none of the temperament of the Virgin Queen. She was, on the contrary, the very soul of consideration; her manners could be almost awesomely good. When Osborne heard in church

Christ's commandment "Be ye perfect, even as your father in heaven is perfect," he would reflect that only Sophonisbe had obeyed.

It was like her, too, to have been born without wisdom teeth or an appendix. She had sprung into the world like Athena from the brain of Zeus, armed with helmet and spear, ready for action; nothing had to be removed or replaced. Even her hair, a fine rusty red, worn in high curls, had shown not a single grey unit right up to her present fifty-second year, nor was there any line in her marble-skinned, oblong, high-cheeked face, nor any stoop in her erect slim figure or stumble in her quick stride. Sophonisbe was admittedly not a beautiful woman — *noble* was the better word for her — and she might even have been said to have what the military call "command presence," had such a term been compatible with the openness and charm of her outgoing personality. It sometimes occurred to Osborne that the world — including himself — was waiting to see if it could catch Sophonisbe in an imperfection: some showing of a sense of even mild superiority, or perhaps something as small as a claim of expertise in a field where she was at best an amateur, but if so, they waited in vain. Those clear-gazing, all-seeing, blue-green eyes would never have to be cast down in abashment or shame.

It had not always been so. As a girl Sophonisbe had been plainer and more muted, an adored only child who nonetheless seemed to pull back from the glittering destiny that her devoted widower father dangled before her undazzled eyes and who turned instead to the guidance of the then slimmer and handsomer older cousin who dwelt next door. Touched by the child's — and later the young woman's — constant fidelity to all of his views, Osborne had adapted himself easily and gracefully to the role of chosen mentor, for which indeed, in the decade following his majority, he had ample leisure, having elected, with full parental and avuncular approval, to eschew the family business in favor of becoming an amateur of the arts.

The change in their relative roles had come with a startling, almost a shattering swiftness. At thirty-one Osborne had, not uncomplacently, deemed himself hopelessly in love with a society beauty who was safely out of his range, being herself hopelessly enamored of a matinée idol. It was Sophonisbe who, without having previously once referred to his supposedly fatal passion, put an end to it with one devastating comment.

"It's all nonsense, you know," she announced to him gravely. "You're wasting your time in the wildest of goose chases. For if you ever caught your goose — which, incidentally, is just what your inamorata is — you'd be the first to regret it. Leave her to her silly actor. He's on the skids, and when he realizes it, he'll come round. He needs her money, and you don't."

"And where the devil did you learn all this?" Osborne demanded, aghast.

"I've made it my business to find out."

"And just why, if I may ask, am I *your* business?"

"Because it's always been in the cards that you should marry no one but me."

And so apparently it had been. Osborne's uncle had decided at last that his nephew was the right man to be entrusted with the destiny of his gifted but unpredictable daughter. Osborne was not only obviously favored by Sophonisbe; he was tactful and good-tempered, and he would have a fortune sufficient to exempt him from mercenary motives. And what the elder Renwick brother decided, the younger was bound to approve. Osborne had some feeling that his life was being taken out of his hands, but what, he had the good sense to ask himself, had that life really amounted to? Anything more than a decade of dabbling in art and an unrequited love? It was time that he settled down.

With the marriage of the cousins the two

widower Renwicks seemed to have said their *nunc dimittis,* for they did not survive it long. Left alone with their new riches, Osborne and his bride faced a welcoming world — and each other. Sophonisbe seemed to have left her chrysalis at the altar and become, as it were, overnight the splendid lepidopteran she must have always been destined to be. Osborne had almost fallen in love with her on their honeymoon in Morocco; the fine freedom of her embracements in no way recalled the quiet girl of her father's gloomy mansion. But a trouble was born in their very ardor, perhaps one inevitable for a man of his previous inhibitions: he never had the feeling that he really possessed her.

He sought to imagine himself an Endymion wooed by Selene, but this fantasy, though at first seductive, contained the germ of its own destruction: a mortal could never really "have" the moon. Even at the pitch of orgasm, she seemed to escape him. Yet the real Sophonisbe manifested no disappointment with his ardor; on the contrary, she appeared to derive satisfaction from it. There was never anything so crude as a reproach for the inadequacy of his performance, yet her continued barrenness reinforced his sense of her essential impregnability to his efforts. When, some dozen years later, their lovemaking having become much less frequent, they retired at last, by a kind of tacit mutual consent, to separate bed chambers, it was as if the gods of her higher world had nodded their silent approval of the restoration of Selene's chastity. But he was left to the bitterness of the inevitable male reaction that such a lunar eclipse might have been caused by what his Olympian "in-laws" may have seen as his clumsy pawing.

Yet he had always to concede that no wife could have striven harder to induce him to make more of himself, and never, either, with any vulgar suggestion that he should "shake a leg." Whenever he accomplished something, she would simply radiate with a delight that he couldn't miss, but that was never tastelessly effusive. Thus she had greeted the success of his little book of aphorisms à la Rochefoucauld which had caught and held the attention of the *cognoscenti* for so many years. It was only after its third printing that she indulged herself in the ordering of a private edition on vellum, sumptuously bound in morocco, and limited to 250 copies. She had shown a similar tact and reticence before according the same treatment to his memoirs of his childhood, admired by no less a critic than H. L. Mencken, and his single novel, *You That Look Pale*, which had been optioned for a movie but never made. His watercolors of the interiors of the pleasanter houses of their friends she had displayed at a show at her own museum, and she always insisted that he accompany on the piano any singer at one of her charity concerts. He was too diffident to offer his own services in this latter respect, but he appreciated her recognition that his musical talents were somewhere between those of a top amateur and a professional.

And if she seemed content with what he *had* accomplished, if she did not push him further, like Ulysses, "to sail beyond the western stars" before he died, did that not mean that she justly appreciated his limits? And should he resent that? Of course not! But he did. He wanted desperately to have her believe that he was still capable of "some work of noble note" before the end. Surely she thought *she* was.

And recently he had been entertaining a different kind of jealousy, a more personal one. He had always recognized that he had entered into marriage without passion, counting on hers to be enough for two, but how did he know that hers had not been assumed? Her will power was capable of anything. Had not the very coolness of her proposal to him implied an act of resolution, the iron suppression, perhaps, of some guilty attraction to a social inferior or a married man? She would have done almost anything, he knew, for her father, and her father had favored his nephew. Oh, it was all too possible! Why else would she have acceded so easily to their separate chambers?

And if that were indeed the case, had not the only remarkable thing in his life consisted in his provision of such a task for his remarkable spouse? For his having given her the opportunity to convert her passion for one man into the devoted care of another? How many women could have done *that?* Perhaps the answer to his new dream of creating a great final opus would be to write a book about *her,* a novel presumably, as he would never get the facts from her. Or might he?

Yet the more he toyed with the idea, watching her now even more closely from day to day, clipping flowers in her greenhouse, or seated at her desk, handing pieces of mail to her secretary with brief, precise instructions, or smiling at him across the dining room table as she raised her soup spoon for the initial sip, the more he began to be irked by the suspicion that his book, should he ever write it (anonymously or for posthumous publication?), might signify his ultimate encapsulation into the greater unity of Sophonisbe.

But this kind of speculation couldn't go on.

One morning he summoned up his determination to put his question to her. He had followed her into the garden and waited while she consulted with one of her staff on the state of the begonias that lined the flagstone path to the Temple of Apollo. When she had finished with her man, Osborne suggested that they stroll across the lawn and sit in the shade of the giant weeping purple beech.

"Why, how pleasant!" she exclaimed. "You so rarely walk about the place these days. I had begun to wonder if you're tired of it."

"That would be like being tired of you, my dear. And we know what age cannot wither nor custom stale."

"Isn't it rather my infinite regularity? Isn't that what still intrigues our friends? If it still intrigues them."

She could say these things without the least trace of an injured feeling. They were seated now on a wooden bench whose back was slanted and curved for the better comfort of its occupants. Sophonisbe would never tolerate the coldness of marble for human seating. Yet she herself was indifferent to luxury. Everything was designed for the ease of guests. Or was it so that she could glory in having created that ease? Osborne shook his head involuntarily in his own reproof. Was he becoming really nasty?

"No, Sophonisbe." He never abbreviated the name of the Numidian queen. "Let us rather call it your infinite harmoniousness. There has to be a sublime variety as the basis of that. If I've remained more indoors in recent months, it may be that I've reached the age where the mind does most of the roaming. I'm quite happy reading in the library with a window open to your beautiful garden."

"And where, my dear, does your mind roam?"

"All over, as minds do. But recently it has been frisking about you and your wonderful life."

"About *me?* But you know all about me."

"Ah, but do I? Edith Wharton said of her heroine Lily Bart that she must have cost a great deal to make, that a great many dull and ugly people may have been sacrificed to produce her. I don't think that of you, of course. You couldn't have tolerated any unkindness, even in your own creation. I think a good many beautiful people might have gone into your making, but they were surely not sacrificed."

She was amused. "What did happen to them?"

"Perhaps when their function was fulfilled, they simply departed, the better for having been part of the process."

"What sort of people are you talking about?"

"What about some young man? Beautiful, no doubt, as a Greek god. And fine of character, too. Capable of teaching a woman a great love. But not a man, in the end, whom Sophonisbe Renwick could marry."

Her smile faded, but in the brief silence that followed she was more pensive than irked. "Why not?"

"Perhaps he was not free. Or of a lower order."

"Like Michael?"

He was startled. "Michael? Who was Michael?"

Her laugh was good-natured. "Surely, Ozzie, you remember Michael? He was one of Father's footmen. The handsomest man you ever saw! Though I suppose he wouldn't have seemed so beautiful to you. Anyway, you're quite right. I had the most tremendous crush on Michael. I almost contemplated suicide when he told us he was engaged to *your* father's kitchen maid."

"You aren't going to take my idea seriously?"

"Your idea that I may have learned love from a mysterious male admirer? I'm taking it very seriously."

"But is there anything in it?"

"Ah, I shouldn't dream of telling you that! An enigma can be an asset for a woman, particularly an aging woman. But here is Tommy coming across the lawn, no doubt to complain that I haven't been down to his rock garden all this week. Will you come with me to the rock garden, Ozzie dear?"

"No, thank you."

"You'd rather stay here and speculate on my past amours? Well, have a lovely time!"

He felt a thorough fool, which did not improve his souring temper, but he at least gave up the silly notion of seeking romance in the early annals of his chaste spouse. He did not, however, resign himself to his former state of mute admiration. On the contrary, his newly aroused, but no doubt long dormant, curiosity in finding a vulnerable spot in the bright mail that encased her seemed rapidly to be becoming an obsession. He found himself engaging in fantasized conversations with imagined admirers of Sophonisbe in which he wittily exposed her "protective coloration."

The extent to which one of these must have been carefully rehearsed in his mind came out startlingly one night at a dinner party when he heard himself offering this perfectly articulated reply to a question from his neighbor as to whether her "imperturbable hostess" ever "lost her cool":

"Oh, I daresay there must have been eruptions in the past. Before, I mean, she attained what you ladies call 'a certain age.' She has always been, as you can tell from the portrait over the mantel, a passionate admirer of that English monarch, an aspect of whose personality was her unviolated sexual state. I refer, of course, to the prince (she preferred the male designation) who is sometimes described by certain genealogically ambitious Bostonians as 'Cousin Bessie Tudor.' Well, a less known aspect of that sovereign's personality was that Mother Nature, stingy in her respect, endowed her with only three menstrual periods a year, each one, presumably, having to make up in its turbulence for a missing three. Her temper in these weeks may be imagined, and any courtier who wished to keep his head on his shoulders did well to retire to his country estate. Now whether my good wife in her earlier days ever emulated her model by boxing the ears or slapping the faces of her waiting women, I have no way of telling, as her conduct with me has always been irreproachable. I merely throw out the possibility."

He now saw in the pursed lips and averted eyes of the lady addressed how deeply he had shocked her. Was that what he had wanted? Had he become one of those elderly epicures, usually bachelors, finely tailored but arid of skin and heart, who express their envious contempt for the sexual delights they have missed by the prosy precision with which they discourse on scatological topics? Hadn't he always despised such?

It hardly surprised him that it was only a matter of days before his little dissertation on the Virgin Queen came to Sophonisbe's attention. No one knew better than he how little color of excuse even the best of friends will need to bring an unflattering remark to its subject's ear.

She brought the matter up at breakfast, a meal they always shared, dressed for the day, in a bay window of the dining room looking out at the rose garden. She had waited till the butler withdrew.

"Amelia Torrance tells me that you offered her some interesting gynecological information the other night."

"That old pussy cat! She couldn't wait to blab it all, could she? I'm afraid a splitting headache and an extra cocktail led to my making an ass of myself. I'm sorry, dear. Please forgive me."

Oh, those blue-green eyes! How they took him in. So serene, so unfooled.

"An extra cocktail? Ozzie, how unlike you. And a splitting headache? But you seemed in rare form that night."

"Pain can be a challenge. I suppose Amelia excused herself on the plea that you had to be warned about my vicious tongue."

"On the contrary, it was you she was worried about. She thought that when a gentleman of your courtly manners started talking in that fashion, it might be the symptom of some inner disturbance."

"Oh, she thought I was bonkers, did she?"

"Nothing so extreme. She thought it might be some kind of hypertension."

"And what do you think?"

"Oh, I've thought that for some time. You have not been quite yourself my darling. And I think I know the reason. It's me."

"I," he could only mutter in his surprise at her intuition.

"I, of course. Thank you. You have been feeling that life has somehow passed you by and left me with all the honor cards. It's not true, of course; those feelings rarely are. But they are there, nonetheless, and they can be very damaging. So the question is, what do we do about it?"

He stared at her with a new wonderment. "You beat everything, Sophonisbe. Tell me your plan. I suppose you have one."

"Oh, yes, I have one. I shouldn't have spoken at all if I hadn't. I have been turning over in my mind all the many things you have done. Should you embark on a new book? A new series of watercolors? Should you write your autobiography? Plan a series of private piano recitals? But the trouble with your present state of mind is that you'd be comparing anything you did with something you're bound to think you'd done better in the past. You must strike out in a new field. I thought you might form a collection. You've helped me with mine, and wonderfully, but you've never done one on your own."

After a considerable pause he asked, simply, "A collection of what?"

"Oh, you would have to choose that. And without a single word of advice from me. That would be the whole point, don't you see? I shouldn't even pay for it. Not a penny! You would use your own money, all of it, if necessary. Or if you were afraid of being dependent on me when the collection was finished, you could protect yourself by buying an annuity now. I understand you can get excellent rates at your age."

Even as he sat there, silent, sunk, sick with shame at the thought of how shabbily in his cheap dinner chat he had treated this generous woman, he began to feel, stealing slowly over him, the first faint waves of the incoming tide of her wonderful idea. What did he have?

Three millions? Three millions to spend when the world was for sale!

Sophonisbe could see that he was becoming intrigued. "Of course, you'd have to travel to find your things. I assume you wouldn't limit yourself to stamps or doorknobs!"

"Oh, we can roam the world!" he exclaimed.

"Not we. You. Don't forget it's of the essence of my plan that you do it alone!"

He took Sophonisbe at her word — there was never any other way to take her — and set off for London, Paris, Berlin and Rome, camping luxuriously in palace hotels for weeks at a time and arranging to be escorted to galleries, auction houses, private collections and even to museums secretly willing to consider "deaccessioning" by avid dealers who charged themselves with the cost of his limousines and fabulous lunches and whom he took a near pleasure in disappointing.

For the more treasures that were piled up before him, the more, like the giant Fasolt in *Das Rheingold*, did he peer through the chinks and crannies to determine whether the reproachful (as he now fancied it) countenance of his wronged wife had been blocked out. For only by bringing back art as peerless as herself could he hope to redeem himself for his petty envy of her superiority to his petty self.

No, he did not want the usual things, the glorious monuments of superstition: missals, canticles and books of hours, gorgeously illuminated in jewelled covers; precious panes of old stained glass; golden reliquaries quaintly wrought; nor those emblems of might: the painted or sculpted likenesses of monarchs, popes and peers, and the gilded furnishings of their habitations. He even turned away from the shimmering landscapes and seascapes of the French Impressionists which covered the walls and advertised the wealth of contemporary tycoons, as well as the manuscripts of classic authors in the possession of which mortal readers sought vainly to approach the divine fire of genius. Osborne hardly knew what he wanted, but he was sure that it had to be very pure, very simple and absolutely true.

He turned his steps now to Greece, though the land had already been plundered. Lord Elgin a century before had taken off the Parthenon the metopes and figures that might have answered his purpose. But he did find in a museum in Olympia a marble stele of which he was told it might be possible to discover a near twin. The decedent whom it commemorated in *bas* relief was a grave-faced youth, wonderfully strong and handsome, shown in profile, full length, clad in a short tunic which exposed his extended right arm and muscular legs. He was clasping the hand of an equally grave older man, a bearded father or tutor, whose expression of sadness might have been eased by the prospect of an early reunion with the lost son or pupil. The radiated air of stillness, of calm, of a stoical acceptance of the extinction of love and beauty was unutterably moving to Osborne. It conveyed the feeling that even if life were preceded and followed by nothingness, it was still a marvellous thing to have had, and that the young athlete or scholar or warrior, or whatever he had been, with the devoted hound at his heels had certainly had it.

To find other such steles, or even one, he resolved to wander over all of Attica, Ionia and Magna Graecia, if necessary, and to accompany him he employed an expert Athenian guide who was reputed to know every outlet of Greek statuary. He found many steles, of children and of adults, old and young, some so defaced as to be barely recognizable, some crude, some even banal, but in the end he purchased only six, these, however, of what he considered a surpassing beauty, though none the equal of the Olympian masterpiece. It was time, anyway, to go home. He had been abroad four months, and Sophonisbe's letters, though patient, were beginning to show a guarded concern.

On the voyage home aboard the *Berengaria* he suffered a stroke which paralyzed much of his left side. Sophonisbe met the ship with an ambulance and drove him straight to a clinic in New Jersey. She sat beside his stretcher and listened carefully as he tried to articulate the words to describe the stele that he wished to be placed over his tomb. This, however, turned out not to be necessary, as he was able to come home after a six months' stay and a therapeutical course which partly restored movement to his damaged arm and leg.

The first day that he was allowed out of the house in his wheelchair, Sophonisbe announced a special treat. He was to be conducted by his valet to the new garden where she had set up his steles.

"Oh, I see by that look, my dear, that you wonder that they should have been put outside. Never fear. They will be taken into a special shelter at the first hint of cold weather, a beautiful shed which is a kind of tiny museum in itself. And my orders are explicit that they are to be covered with canvas at the first drop of rain. And no, I shan't go with you on your first visit. I don't want you to have to worry about my seeing any reaction that you may have."

Tim, his faithful valet of thirty years, wheeled him slowly through the grounds to the new plot. Sophonisbe had taken for her model the *gardino segreto* of the Villa Giulia in Rome and enclosed an oblong space of rose parterres, arbors and turf seats in a yellow wall punctuated by six entablatures with chaste triangular cornices supported by Ionic columns, under each of which reposed one of his steles.

It was perfect. It was the cemetery of which the sculptors might have dreamed.

But it was something more. As he was wheeled slowly from one stele to another, it came over him with a chilling, deadly certainty that the garden was too good for his purchased art. His steles seemed pale, crumbled, forlorn. Brought up in front of the sixth and last, he finally allowed his dismay to erupt.

"They're not good enough, are they, Tim? Not good enough for this garden, anyway. Don't try to fool me. I'm right, aren't I?"

"But what could you do, sir? All the best ones were already in museums. Madam said that under the circumstances you did extraordinarily well. And certainly no Greek things anywhere have a finer setting."

"And no man has a finer setting than I, isn't

that so, Tim? Wasn't I born to be placed in the right setting by Mrs. Renwick? To be improved by her? Even to be excused by her?"

"I don't know what you mean by that, sir. All I know is that Madam really slaved over this garden. She practically selected every pebble in the footpaths!"

Osborne nodded and made no further comment. On the way back to the house he reflected that it appeared to be his destiny to be loved and cherished as few men were. He certainly did not deserve it; he had not even desired it. Sophonisbe's love had consumed him. Obliterated him? As the queen bee disposes of her mate? But wasn't it possible, after all, that providing an object for Sophonisbe's love was a destiny quite as worthy of him as any he could have fashioned for himself without her? Wasn't he a part, even perhaps a vital part, of her whole wonderful existence? Could she have done without him all the things she had done?

"I think I'll sit on the terrace for a bit, Tim."

"Mrs. Renwick said you were not to be out more than half an hour, sir. We're already over that."

"Very well, Tim. Take me in."

The Poetaster

1

As I refuse to have any visitors, even my children or my separated but still compassionate spouse, and as I find it impossible to read the detective stories which were so long my staple, and as music makes me fretful, I have decided to act on Dr. Burns's suggestion that I write out my reactions to what has happened to me. He thought I might find it easier to dictate, but as I cannot endure the idea of any ear, even that of a machine, hearing what I have to say, I am constrained to use a pencil. The written word has the advantage of being easily disposed of, should the urge seize me. And I can stroll about my bedroom and sitting room as I compose sentences in my mind, or walk out on the ample balcony and survey the beautiful autumnal Connecticut landscape and breathe in the fresh air that can never now cleanse me. I am even free to leave the building and ramble in the wide grounds of the sanatorium, for none of the injured parties to my appalling conduct have seen fit to prosecute, and the district attorney of Suffolk

County in Long Island has dropped his charges. But I still cannot face the glances of my fellow inmates. I fear I shall read scorn even in the eyes of the victims of Alzheimer's, who must be unaware of my shame, indeed, of my very identity.

This is not my first visit to Golden Hill, that most appropriate name for this luxurious asylum for rich alcoholics, depressives and mindless antiquities. My forty-two years of existence have been punctuated by recurrent nervous breakdowns, one approximately every half-dozen years, starting as early as my freshman year at Yale, but until now they were all softened by the sympathy of family and friends; none lasted more than a few months, and each ended in a complete recovery. It was not even considered unusual that an industrialist of my importance and responsibilities should occasionally crack under the strain of grueling work and grave market and labor problems; perhaps it added a sympathetic gloss to the sternness of my public image. But any compassion aroused by my current breakdown must inevitably be composed of only one part charity and at least three parts contempt. We learned at school that Greek tragedy is premised on the fall of a great man from a great height. And Attic tragedy is made more poignant if the protagonist's fate be unseemly as well as cruel, such as Oedipus's discovery that he has married his own mother. But suppose that it is worse than unseemly, suppose it is disgusting, even ludicrous, leaving no room for awe or tears, but evoking simply a shudder, a grimace, a turning away, never to look back again?

Well! As Dr. Burns says, it may be something to have touched bottom. But that is on the assumption that the rest of the way is up. Suppose there is no way up? Suppose there is no way of regaining, even in the sexually liberated atmosphere of the 1950s, my self-respect and honor? Oh, I daresay if I were young, anything might be forgiven me, but I am forty-two, and will be judged even by teen-agers, or should I say especially by them, according to the standards of my own generation. And if, by a miracle, I could induce my contemporaries to forgive me, could I ever forgive myself?

Aye, there's the rub. For I loathe myself. Only the instinctive shrinking from death stands between me and the fatal dose that I have already in my possession. My only hope of preserving any kind of sanity is to attempt a giant step out of myself and to focus my mental vision on a kind of private screening of my own life story.

There can be no better start than to place

squarely on the desk before me this newspaper clipping which I have alone saved from the sordid pile.

"The summer colony at Southampton has been greatly shocked (to put it mildly) to learn at last the identity of the lewd telephone caller. The debutantes of the season will no longer have to ask their fathers or brothers to pick up the ringing instrument at their bedside. The man who purred his pornographic greetings through a handkerchief is none other than Hugh Hammersly, president of Hammersly Mills, the furniture and carpet tycoon, who, separated from his wife, Nancy, has been spending the summer alone in his big rented villa on the dunes. The police suspected that the dirty mouth belonged to a summer resident, as all of his targets were young ladies of noted families whose trim and scantily clad figures the blue-blooded lecher must have ogled at the beach club, but it was not until one of the Hammersly servants, picking up the telephone 'below stairs' to make a personal call, heard her master on the same line that . . ."

The same story had run in every journal and been rehashed in the weekly news magazines. I have little doubt that the crooked leaders of the unions which I have fought so bitterly and so successfully all these years on behalf of their deluded workers have had a hand in spreading the good news. But was it necessary? What is more eagerly lapped up by a scandal-loving public than the tumble from grace of a model of virtue and propriety? What did decades of a blameless life amount to in opposition to a single week of folly? My good deeds are all wiped out; I am reduced to a cartoon of a satyr leering into his telephone.

Poor Hughie Junior and Lisa! Will they be able to bear the sneers, hidden or open, at Buckley and Chapin? I couldn't face the poor darlings, even if they were allowed to come up here to show their concern. And my mother . . . no, no, it's out of the question. Thank God for my money, which can seal all my doors and provide me with private guards if it comes to that. Oh, horror . . .

I had to break off to take a sedative. Now I am calm again. I can take a steadier look at the man with the telephone. Was it really I who made those calls? Did I really do it? Certainly the first one was almost involuntary. I had for weeks fought the fantasy of making it, yes. Oh, yes, I have always had licentious fantasies — who hasn't? But they recently became exhaustingly real. Out of my loneliness last summer, my missing Nancy so sorely, out of my isolation from old friends, my feeling that everyone perversely misunderstood me, "out of my weakness and my melancholy," as Hamlet put it, the devil, "as he is very potent with such spirits," may have devised this trick to damn me. I can just barely recall, after a fourth solitary cocktail one lonely evening, dialing Laura Westfall's number and being startled when the girl herself answered the ring.

And then . . .

But stop. My purpose is not to wallow in my own piss. No, I must go back and back. I must learn to be my own analyst.

What is very clear to me at the outset is that I have always been two persons. I do not mean that I am a schizophrenic, a psychic split personality. I mean that quite consciously I have always been two distinct individuals. Perhaps this is partially true of everyone; my case may be only a matter of degree. One Hugh Hammersly has been a yearning romantic, a dreamer, a would-be poet or artist of some sort. The other has been a hard-headed, practical man of affairs. My preference was to be the first, but life has inexorably molded me into the second.

Romance from the beginning was exemplified by my family's summer home in Rhinebeck on the Hudson, where my grandfather, the first Hugh and the founder of our fortune, had commissioned Alexander Jackson Davis to erect, on top of a hill overlooking the mighty waterway, a Gothic castle of grey local rock with a massive, machicolated round tower, high peaked gables and oriel windows. Available for my solitary rambles were some thousand acres of the finest forest and pasture land, a stable, a cattle farm and two miles of glorious riverbank. I was perfectly happy to amuse myself alone, never inviting my schoolmates from the city for a weekend, or sharing my excursions with my stout, plain, admiring but shunned younger sister, contenting myself with the occasional vassalage of two of my juniors on the estate, sons of the superintendent and the head gardener. These were respectfully willing to play minor roles in the games that I invented of knights of yore, sometimes attacking and sometimes defending the castle on high. My parents were entirely willing to let me do as I chose, sublimely confident that the open air and the countryside were all that a healthy lad could need. I had little occasion to adapt myself to the tastes or needs of my contemporaries.

At least in Rhinebeck. In New York, on lower Madison Avenue, we occupied a gloomy French Renaissance château, also built by my grandfather, whose only and submissive child my father had been, and I attended Miss Kate Bovee's school for boys. There, as later at Chelton School in Massachusetts and at Yale, I achieved top grades, excelling particularly in courses requiring precision and exactitude, like mathematics and Latin grammar, and I got on well enough with my classmates, though I formed no intimacies and occasionally had to protect my preferred isolation with perhaps too ready fists. My soul was always at Rhinebeck, where our hills and dales and the great moving river did not have to be shared with inanely laughing or inanely jeering or even inanely smutty boys.

My parents no doubt had much to do with my love of solitude. Mother certainly showed little need of intimates, though she rose adequately to the performance of social duties. She was the lofty priestess around whom her households in town and country silently and efficiently moved. I think of her as somehow "swathed," clad in simple but flowing garments, even in an era of "flappers" (of whose very existence she seemed unaware), pale, remote, ethereal but very much in charge, with an eye for the least domestic disorder and a low but inexorable voice to utter her gentle but instantly obeyed commands. Mother was a poetess (she would never have called herself a poet); she wrote haunting love lyrics privately printed in small, beautifully bound volumes. I know that sounds esoteric, but she could have had them published — several known editors had asked for them. But Mother had no interest in the public.

It is odd, I suppose, that it never occurred to me until now that Mother's romantic idylls were clearly not inspired by Father, or indeed by any identifiable male. She and Father had a relationship of the highest mutual respect and consideration; I never heard them exchange a harsh or bitter word. Yet he appeared in many ways more her major domo than her spouse; she seemed to regard him and his mills (towards which she maintained a total, perhaps a rather disdainful indifference) as the necessary means of supporting the atmosphere most nourishing to her genius. His function in life was necessarily on a lower plane than hers. This, she would no doubt have conceded, was not in any way his fault; it might even have been his glory. It was, anyway, the way things were.

Father, for his part, perfectly comprehended her attitude, but there was no humility in his acceptance of it. He seemed if anything gently amused. He had been reared by a demanding and tyrannical sire, and he had accommodated himself to the old tycoon's wishes with a tact and understanding which had adequately preserved his own integrity. He was a handsome man with thick hair which, like my own, seemed to have been always grey, and a fine aquiline nose that was somehow out of key with his smiling blue eyes. He could never have been the industrial pioneer his father had been, but he was the perfect caretaker, the efficient carrier-on of a business once started. That he lived in both of his father's houses after the latter's death was simply the continuation of an accepted routine; we had all lived with Grandpa before.

Towards myself his attitude was loving, complimentary and at times a bit apprehensive.

"You've got your grandfather's brain," he often told me. "And a far better instrument than mine. No, no, you needn't shake your head. I know what I'm talking about, and I never flatter, least of all a dear son. You have a head for figures and the memory of an elephant. You might take over the mills and build them into something greater than I've been able to. But I don't want you ever to feel that that's what you have to do. I want you to have your own life, my boy. If you don't have that, what do you have?"

And he spoke as one who knew.

Well, I certainly had no intention at that time of going into the family business. It was not that I looked down upon it, as I suspected Mother of doing. I had often accompanied Father on his tours of inspection of our mills and factories, and I had made myself thoroughly familiar with the mechanics of the trade at an early age. I knew how to operate planers, cutters and rip saws, and I had learned the arts of antiquing and even of rug weaving. Everyone agreed that I had a natural aptitude for the furniture business. But I still saw myself as my mother's child, and my future as something in the arts, a writer, perhaps even a poet. I believe that Father from the beginning had his doubts about this, but he knew me well enough to know that I would have to find it out for myself.

It is a pity that I did not make more of Father's love for me, for it was considerably stronger than Mother's. Mother cared for me and Doris in her own way, but her way was a rather cool one. As her offspring, we were entitled to her tolerating smiles, her mild kisses and her exceedingly penetrating insights. Oh, she knew us both! Her encomiums and reprimands were couched in the same soft, never-to-be-ignored tone.

Her essential detachment was revealed to me with painful clarity on the day I submitted for her criticism a sonnet of mine which, to my intense pride, had been accepted by the

Cheltonian, the student paper of the Massachusetts boarding school to which I had been sent for my last three pre-college years. The poem described the romantic ruin of a medieval castle as an example of the futility of all human endeavor. I was particularly proud of the final couplet:

The sound of ravens beating with their
  wings
On lofty casements of this hall of kings.

"Ravens wouldn't beat against the windows," Mother pointed out. "Why should they, unless they wanted to get in? They're very intelligent birds, you know. And they could see there was nothing inside for them. Besides, wouldn't the windows have been smashed? That's the first thing vandals do."

I was distressed at how little the poetess and how much the critic was showing. "But it's the overall effect I'm getting at. Don't you see it at all?"

"No. In poetry the detail is everything. And do you remember Mr. Low's old castle in Garrison? Every window was broken after it had been left unoccupied for only two years. It would happen here too."

Our little dialogue was taking place in Rhinebeck during a Christmas vacation. I shuddered at the mere idea of vandals in the beloved house and took the sonnet from her to stuff in my pocket.

"It could never happen here," I said firmly.

"Why on earth not?"

"Because we'd never leave the house empty."

"Your parents can't live forever, my child. And this place would be much too big for you or Doris to maintain after you'd paid all the death duties."

"I'd live here if I had to do all the work on the place myself!"

Mother looked at me quizzically. "Does it really mean that much to you? Well, you might not be reduced to such straits. Your father thinks you'll make a great businessman. Concentrate on practical things, my child, and forget about sonnets and maybe you'll have a greater place than this one day."

"But I want to write sonnets! I want to make beautiful things!"

"Ah, what we want, my dear. How many of us get that?"

"But you have! You've written beautiful things. And hasn't that been what you've cared about more than anything in the whole world?"

Mother looked suddenly grave. She seemed to be pondering my question as if she were willing to face up to its every implication. "Yes, child," she answered at last in what struck me as a tone of something almost like defiance. "I really believe it has been."

2

I was moderately content at Chelton School, which I attended from the ages of fifteen to seventeen. It was easy enough for me to adapt to a rigid routine; I had always been a kind of classical romantic with a faith in order as the guardian of dreams. At Rhinebeck I keenly appreciated the well-prepared, silently served meals in the great cool dining hall after my day-long rambles in the wild. The school system of formally conducted classrooms, organized athletics and regular chapel services, all announced by constantly ringing bells, struck me as the only practical way of maintaining any sort of order and decorum among four hundred essentially lawless young males.

It is obvious from the above that I did not care for my classmates any more than I had cared for them at Bovee. I was neither good-looking nor outstandingly athletic, two near essentials for popularity in a boys' boarding school, but I was stocky and strong, and when the crowd in my dormitory found that, although I was odd enough to enjoy solitary walks on weekends, I otherwise conformed to school norms of behavior, they left me largely alone. I say "largely" because there was one lurid incident that demonstrated only too vividly the revenge that the gregarious will take, given the opportune occasion, on the isolated soul.

I made one friend, however: Eric Potter. He was a tall, fair-haired youth whose striking good looks and athletic ability would have made him one of the leaders of our form had he shown the slightest interest in being that. He was not as stand-offish as I; he tolerated the crowd, but he had no relish for it. Without disapproving openly of school goals, without any apparent wish to be a rebel, he nonetheless stood apart from the clatter and chatter of institutional loyalties and animosities. He was more like a master than a student; he seemed maturer than the rest of us; his manners were civil but only marginally so. Yet his prowess on the football field assured him of the respect of those who deplored or even resented his aloofness.

He came of a poor branch of an old Boston family and was on a partial scholarship, but he took such good care of his few possessions, his clothes in particular, that he always appeared trimmer and better dressed than any of his richer and more ragged classmates. Watching him in the football field and in the boxing ring, or sitting by himself, as he sometimes chose to do, on a marble bench in the chapel garth gazing at the distant hills, I likened him to a Byronic hero, such as the lonely and proud Corsair living apart from the rowdy pirates who adored him and whom he ruled. Could this be the friend I might have been waiting for so long, the worthy companion of my forest rambles, the sharer of my ideals and aspirations? For all my reticence, I was not shy; I was bold enough to thrust myself on Eric.

He did not reject my overtures; he was perfectly willing to chat if I dropped into his study after evening work hours, though he did not hesitate to tell me if he preferred to read or go up to the dormitory master's rooms to listen to classical music. But I began to make progress when we discovered that we were on different sides of the political fence. We were then in the depth of the Great Depression; I was the blackest of Republicans; he, the pinkest of Democrats. Eric was disgusted with my ideas, but he seemed to regard it as his tedious duty to straighten me out. His disgust turned into something more like anger when I argued that the National Labor Relations Act was unconstitutional.

"The only way an employer can prove that he's bargained fairly," I insisted, "is by making some concession in each case. And suppose he's really up against it? Suppose he can't make any at all without going in the red?"

"Oh, my God, Hammersly, what a pig of a boss's brat you are! Your old man could make a hundred concessions and still grind a fat profit out of the sweat of his serfs. And why would he have to, anyway? Hasn't he bust every union that tried to organize his sacred plants?"

I smiled. I always liked to see an opponent in argument lose his temper. Father had taught me the principle of true conservatism: it is never necessary to get hot when you know you're right. "My father does more for his workers than any union possibly could. Keeping unions out of his business has saved him enough money to enable him to keep two mills running that are losers. He does it just to preserve the jobs!"

"Which proves he could make concessions if he was unionized!"

"Which proves he has made them already. Who needs a union? My father preserves a just ratio between overhead and profit. Why should he allow anyone to meddle with it? Particularly unions run by racketeers!"

Eric stared at me for a moment in bafflement and then gave it up. "What a bloody royalist you are, Hammersly. I guess there's no point arguing with you. Anyway, I don't suppose it'll matter to you when you're sitting in your villa on the Riviera writing sonnets. Just so long as the dividends keep rolling in."

"I shan't be writing sonnets. I've given up poetry. I shall be writing prose. Beautiful prose, I hope, like Benjamin Disraeli's. But the business will always matter to me. I expect to have my full share in management."

"How can you do that and be a writer?"

"Disraeli wrote a whole shelf of novels and still became prime minister of England."

"And you think you're another Disraeli?"

"Why not?"

"Well, God help the workers if that's so. I'll say this for you. If vanity is an asset, you're not a bloated millionaire in rugs alone. Now scram and let me finish my who-done-it."

Yet our very differences contributed to our friendship. Eric found me impossible but amusing. He continued to tolerate me, and I, never having had a real friend before, was quite satisfied with the mild affection he offered. I listened intently when he talked about his family, his hobbies, his ambitions, though the latter struck me as rather paltry for so noble a soul. Eric professed to be more interested in "living" than in any particular accomplishment.

"Oh, I'll probably end up like my dad as a customer's man, buying and selling securities for bloated fat cats like you. I won't need too much dough. Enough for a couple of rooms and a shack on the dunes for summers. Or maybe a log cabin in the Maine woods."

"Your wife is going to want more than that."

"I doubt that I'll marry. I don't see myself as a family man. I'll need a gal now and then, but that's another matter."

Eric was supposed to be very "advanced" in these matters. There was a school rumor that he had "had" one of the maids in the drying room in our dormitory cellar. I never asked him about this and was rather disgusted at the esteem it rated him. It may, however, have been his sexual maturity that enabled him to help me in a horrid incident that now occurred.

I found myself alone one afternoon in my form's locker room in the gymnasium after a workout with weights. I had always detested public nudity, and I would wait, if feasible (which it usually wasn't), until the showers were empty, or partly so, and then proceed to them, stripped, but with a towel firmly tied about my loins. But on that day, for some reason, perhaps because of the unusual vacancy of the place, I left the towel behind and strode to the scene of my ablutions with an unwonted and certainly unjustified male pride in my bare physique, perhaps conceiving myself as some kind of Tarzan, lord of a jungle in which he had no human rivals. The trickle of water on my shoulders and down my back was suddenly titillating and erogenous, and I found myself subject to a very stiff erection.

It was dangerous; it was exciting; and then . . .

It was appalling.

For from the other side of the shower room I heard the noise of a suddenly arriving hockey team, who had already stripped and were hurrying to the showers. There was no place I could get to in time, and of course I had no cover. And the chamber was soon filled with naked boys who shrieked with glee and pretended scandalization when they spied my condition and proceeded to pelt me with soap and snap towels at my legs and behind.

I was completely paralyzed with horror and mortification. I could make not even a gesture in my own defense, nor could I run away. How long this hellish pandemonium would have lasted I cannot tell, but it was interrupted by a tall bare figure who dashed into the crowd using his towel with such stinging effect that my persecutors retreated. As soon as the entrance to the room had been cleared, he hissed at me to "scram," which, needless to say, I did, though the cause of my shame had now disappeared. Of course my savior was Eric. My gratitude was almost obliterated by my dismay that he should have witnessed my humiliation. I hurried to the locker room, dressed and returned to my dorm.

To my eternal gratitude Eric never referred to the incident. This almost made up for the fact that every other boy in our form did.

Sixth form year — our final one at Chelton — was filled with the pleasant anticipation of the freer life that college would open up for us. Fifteen of our class were chosen to be monitors, boys charged with the task of assisting the faculty in the running of the school and endowed with disciplinary powers over the lower forms. They were theoretically elected by the outgoing and incoming sixth forms, but the headmaster notoriously juggled the elections, which was why two such stand-aparts as Eric and I were nominated; he for his athletic record and I for my high marks. I suspect that our clerical, very devout and not always practical headmaster counted on me to assist him in the complicated matter of reorganizing the tangled calendar of school events, and I may add that he was not disappointed. Some of my changes are still in effect today at Chelton.

The incident in the shower room, which had occurred in fifth form year, had by now passed out of every mind but mine, where it lurked as luridly as if it had happened only the week before. But I never admitted to anyone, even Eric, how deeply I hated those who had so humiliated me. I had not been able to identify all my attackers — the raid was too crowded and rushed — but for fear of omitting any I included our whole form, except Eric, in my mental anathema. I even came to associate their desire to expose and mock my shameful nudity with a form of perversion, closely related to what those same boys might do when they sometimes visited each other in cubicles illegally at night after lights.

When I tried to discuss this with Eric, he would only shrug and retort, "What do you expect when they keep boys in a monastery?" But I was sure that he himself never went in for such behavior. There was even a new rumor, though I never quite believed it, that he had also "made" a nurse in the infirmary while occupying one of the few private rooms there because of a supposedly infectious flu.

Girls had so far played little or no role in my emotional life — except for Nancy Van Pelt, whom I shall come to later — and I was far too intelligent and well read not to suspect, with however much dismay, that the considerable role which the handsome image of Eric played in my fantasies borrowed some of its force from the sexual side of my nature. But I clung to the faith that I had never wanted to "do" anything with Eric. I had learned about the *id* and how some curious imp or devil had endowed us with the cesspool of a subconscious mind, but I conceived it a man's duty to keep that subconscious as *sub* as humanly possible. And indeed, was I not right? Look what happened to me in middle age when it erupted! In that happier time of my youth, when I was a student of Greek literature and the pet of the dreamy, scholastic headmaster, I could find a high consolation in Plato's concept of a pure and perfect love between two young men.

I had continued my writing, though after the appearance in the *Cheltonian* of the sonnet which Mother derided, I made no further submissions to that periodical. Why should I wish to be read by the boys at Chelton? I began to compose what I considered polished fables about young Spartans or Athenians, in the genre of Anatole France, their debates, their rivalries, their warfare with the Persians, and, of course, their love for one another. I showed some of these to Eric, who snorted and said that if Periclean Greece had been like that he would have deserted to the army of Xerxes.

But a week after this critique an event occurred which demonstrated unpleasantly his insight into my favorite theory. On an inspection of the boot lockers in the cellar of my dormitory building (one of my monitorial duties) I chanced to discover two fourth formers in the boiler room with their pants down doing . . . well, I'm not going to describe what they were doing. That night, in Eric's study, when I mentioned the incident and he asked me gruffly what I planned to do about it, I told him that, of course, I was going to report it to the headmaster.

"You can't mean it!" he exclaimed sharply. "You know he lives in a dream world. He may even kick the poor guys out of school!"

"Would that be my fault?"

"Whose else? No one's making you be such a bastard."

"What would you do?"

"I wouldn't have seen it, in the first place. But if it had been flung in my face that so I had to do something about it, I might have given them each a couple of black marks and chalked it up to skipping chapel. They'd settle for that — don't worry!"

"You don't find what they were doing repulsive?"

"Distasteful, perhaps. To me, anyway. But not morally. Hell, no."

"Isn't it unnatural? Bestial?"

"All sex is bestial. And how can it be unnatural? It was natural for them, evidently."

"Ugh!"

"Look, dummy. What do you think your Greek warriors were up to?"

"Not that, surely!"

"Well, perhaps not that. They'd have graduated to sodomy. Why do you think your darling Plato put such an emphasis on purity? For the same reason our head does, in all those mellifluous sermons. Because it's so damn rare."

I made no report to the headmaster, and I took no other action against the guilty boys. Nor did I again mention my notions of Greek friendship to Eric. I did not even write any more stories about it. In fact, I gave up writing stories altogether. The world seemed determined to repudiate my romanticism.

That spring vacation, our last at Chelton, I saw a lot of Nancy Van Pelt. The Van Pelts were our summer neighbors on the Hudson; they lived in a manor which had been in their family since the Revolution, but they lived in it very frugally, with a single faithful old retainer, for Mr. Van Pelt was one of those foolish and desperate men who went out a window after the failure of his Wall Street brokerage firm in the terrible autumn of 1929. His tall and svelte-figured widow, very chic, with a haggard pale face, the blackest eyes and a wonderful rumbling laugh, was popular and courageous in genteel poverty; she wore the donated old dresses of her richer neighbors and looked infinitely smarter in them than they ever had. She had two sons and a daughter, all three much jollier, rounder and more rubicund than their adored, elegant mother. It was generally predicted that they would make good marriages, and in time they all did. For the Van Pelts supplied the heartiness and cheer at which the rest of the community warmed their cooler fingers.

Nancy, to put it on the line, was simply the nicest and dearest girl I have ever known. She was on the short side, but strong — an excellent athlete — and she had black curly hair, a round smiling face and large earnest blue eyes. She was not so much pretty as enticingly amiable. She was always trying to be bravely sincere and attentive when one talked to her, but she was apt to interrupt with shrieks of uncontrollable laughter. Her mother was forever trying to teach her and her brothers some *tenue,* and then giving it up with an affectionate shrug which seemed to recognize that they could probably be left well enough alone to do things their own way.

Nancy broke through my reserve on occasions with an exuberance that would brook no brush-off. She even succeeded in accompanying me on some of my rustic rambles.

"At least I'll be able to tell Mother I got you to allow me this much," she told me on one of these, when we had paused to sit on the riverbank. "She's always telling me that you're the catch of the neighborhood. And that seventeen isn't a bit too young to start looking!"

"What do you mean, 'catch'?" I asked stiffly.

"Your chips, big boy, what else?" She adopted a comic pose of haughtiness. "Or is that too crass? Should I refer instead to your 'ample revenues'? Or make a slyer reference to your 'responsibilities'?"

"My mother says it's vulgar to talk about money."

"That's when you've got plenty of it and it's new! In our case there's very little of it, but what there is is old. Old? Call it mildewed. So we can talk about it all we like."

I had to be amused. "Does that mean that you're aristocrats?"

"Well, that's what Ma says. She says we have to be something. So she claims there's no one better, at least up here, except perhaps the Livingstons." Nancy raised her snubby nose in mock disdain. "So I'm really rather stooping to be here with you at all."

"You mean the Hammerslys are considered *nouveau riche?* Still?"

"Of course! You have to leave us some weapon. Ma told me that back when she was a girl Mrs. Astor used to say about the Hammerslys, 'Just because we walk on their carpets doesn't mean we have to dine at their table.' " At this, Nancy doubled up with laughter. "Isn't it all a riot? Don't think we wouldn't change our name to Smilkstein for a tiny fraction of what your old man's got!"

Nancy was irresistible; she was also very sexy. She was the first girl who let me kiss her, but she wouldn't have let me do much more even had I tried. She made it clear that we were still just "pals."

"And probably won't ever be much more," she added in a more serious tone. "You claim you're a romantic. Well, so, in my own way, am I. I have my ideals. And I'll probably never meet him."

"Him is an ideal?"

"Why not? My dreamboat. And if I do meet him, he'll probably think me a dog."

Nancy's utter truthfulness had its way of making itself acceptable even when one didn't like it.

It was the custom at Chelton on commencement to have a dance to which the sixth and fifth forms invited girls. I invited Nancy, and she motored up with my parents. Eric had not invited a girl, and I suggested that we attend all the festivities as a trio. It was the mistake of my life. For Nancy discovered she had met her dreamboat a good deal earlier than she had expected.

3

Psychiatrists spend most of their time probing into the dark years of a patient's childhood and adolescence, for that is where all the bad things are supposed to start. Everything, they say, grows out of the early period of our lives, as in a determinist novel, so we are pretty well licked, almost from the beginning. By eighteen, or twenty at the latest, a man is what he is going to be; the rest is consequence or inconsequence. If that be so, the balance of his life — his emotional life, anyway — may be covered in fewer pages than his introduction.

Eric and Nancy's affair was a long time starting. He, like his ancestors, went to Harvard, and Nancy matriculated at Radcliffe, for no other reason, as she later confided in me, than to be as near him as possible. Yet in her first two years there she saw little of him. He apparently felt nothing like the attraction that drew her to him, and it was not until junior year, at a party after a football game, that he started to notice her again.

I went to Yale, but I continued to see Nancy in the summers at Rhinebeck, and on our rambles together she talked frankly and humorously about her seemingly futile quest. It was obvious that any pretensions on my part would be of no avail. I knew that I was falling in love with her, but the facts of the situation kept my feelings under strict control. It was hard for me to imagine that I could ever compete with such a man as Eric; my timid emotion may even have found welcome haven in her obvious preoccupation.

Now, anyway, they were dating each other, and this continued up to and after graduation, when Eric, with his persistent scorn of all commercial life, took the easiest position open to him in the old but unprosperous Potter family brokerage firm. Nancy moved to Boston, taking a stenographer's job in the Fine Arts Museum and living with three Radcliffe friends in a tiny apartment in the Back Bay. Of course, her friends and family began to look for an engagement. Neither she nor Eric had any money, but we all knew that she was far too infatuated to care how humbly she might have to live. Yet still nothing happened. And when war broke out in Europe, it seemed to offer additional excuse for Eric's delay. If indeed he had ever had marriage in mind at all.

After Yale I went to work for Hammersly Mills, in accordance with my old determination to be at all times totally familiar with every detail of the family business, but I was still of a mind not to let this foreclose my resolve to lead a life in some way connected with the arts. I had given up writing, and my painting was strictly amateurish, but there was always the possibility of teaching, or directing a small museum — provided I could contribute sufficiently to its endowment — or becoming a widely wandering observer of beauty the world over. My natural aptitude, however, for business administration almost irked me. Once I put my mind on a particular problem — the opening of a new mill or the shutting down of an obsolete one, the introduction of a new line of cheap home furniture or the revival of an outmoded deluxe one — I could not concentrate on anything else, not even the most interesting new novel or play or the most talked-about art show. My father in less than two years became completely dependent on me. He saw me as the reincarnation of his own father and used to quote his favorite author, the duc de Saint-Simon, about the Grand Dauphin, son of Louis XIV, who had said, when his son was crowned king of Spain, "Now I am the only man in Europe who can refer to the King, my father, and the King, my son, without being a king myself." He knew of my dreams to mix business with art, but he could not believe that such a born manufacturer would ever desert his calling, even temporarily. And has he not been proved right?

What did take me away from the mills, at least for a time, was Pearl Harbor. I had already applied for a naval commission, and after the Japanese attack I was trained for sea duty as a "ninety-day wonder" on the old *Prairie State*, moored on the Hudson. But my own high grades defeated my military ambitions for a year, resulting as they did in my being detained after graduation as a teacher in the same school. Early in 1943, however, I was at last released and promptly applied for duty in the amphibious navy. I had chosen that branch because it was the easiest way for a landlubber to obtain a command; the vessels were clumsy transports, much simpler to handle and maneuver than fighting ships, and I have always operated better when in charge. And when I became skipper of an LST at Camp Bradford, Virginia, leader of a squadron there in training for beaching, I felt all the organizational qualities which I had developed in the mills coalesce into what I liked to think of as a formidable efficiency.

But my real new happiness arose with the sense that the romantic Hugh Hammersly predominated at last. This Hugh would guide his vessel and its crew of a hundred men into the turbulent waters of danger and unload on distant beaches the troops that would destroy our malign foe. Perhaps he would be killed, but that too would be romantic. He was the equal of the dashing marine Lieutenant Potter now, and if he survived the war he might even find a Nancy, disillusioned at last with her nonmarrying lover, ready to listen to his offer of his hand, his heart and his fortune. For I still thought too highly of Eric to regard even his leavings as unworthy of me.

I am afraid that a part of my new image was derived (and once again I am referring to that poem) from "The Corsair." My crew, like that of other LSTs, was far from being the pick of the navy; the better men were assigned to attacking craft. Mine were marginally educated, slow and inclined to be sullen. To convert them into a competent team I devised a system of constant drills: general quarters, fire, man overboard, opening of bow doors, and so forth, at all hours of the day and night, each one of which had to be repeated until it was error proof. I would stand stoically for hours on the bridge, checking by phones and inspecting officers on every detail, and as I saw the ship's company actually beginning to take shape as a unit I felt an exhilarating pride in my own creation. But unlike the lordly and lonely Corsair, I was not beloved by my crew. Indeed, I was hated. But one does not win wars by love and indulgence. Neither do such qualities much serve in business. The average enlisted man or worker has too little stake in victory or monopoly to give his all to the struggle. His loyalty must never be taken for granted; his cooperation must be obtained by discipline.

I was pleased and proud when marine First Lieutenant Potter used a precious few hours of a week's leave to visit me at Camp Bradford. He looked thinner and handsomer as he stood by me on the bridge while I put the ship through its drills. When they were over we went to the wardroom for coffee. I saw that he took note of the fact that the junior officers left when I came in.

"Well?" I asked. "What did you think?"

"A fine show, Captain Bligh."

"Oh, come off it, Eric. That's nothing to what you got in boot camp."

"But with marines it's necessary. Their lives may depend on it. An LST doesn't have to be a goddamn destroyer."

"You mean I should let it be a slop barge?"

"Not at all. There are degrees in everything. Do you *like* people hating your guts?"

"Why should a good officer care about that?"

"A good officer should care about his men."

"Are you giving me lessons in morality, Eric? *You?*"

"What does morality have to do with being a good officer? But let's cut this. I have to be off in a minute, anyway. I came down to talk to you about Nancy. I'm headed for the Pacific, and of course it's in the cards I may not come back."

"That's true of both of us," I retorted, with a perhaps puerile pique.

"Sure, sure. But the odds are better on a ship than on the beach, even if that ship is on the beach. What I'm really getting at is that, killed or not, I don't see myself as

Nancy's future. She ought to marry, and she ought to marry you."

"Because I've got dough?" I asked bitterly.

"Because you can look after her."

"But she loves *you,* Eric."

"She'll get over me. And what's love, in the long run, compared to loyalty? She'll be as true as steel to any man she marries."

"Eric, let me ask you something. Have you ever given a damn about anyone?"

"Perhaps not, as you see it. But I've got an idea of what I may have missed. And I like to clean up my messes. I've always been very neat, you know. I like to think of you and Nancy together. And having put this to you, I've blocked myself from going back to her, even if I *do* survive."

I didn't know what to think. I suppose I was dazed. "Eric, did you ever even *like* me?"

"I liked the non-ass side of you well enough. Work on it."

"I always liked you," I said ruefully.

"That's because you wouldn't face what a heel I was."

He rose now to take his leave. I let him go with little more than a perfunctory farewell. I was still confused. I might have been more responsive had I known that I should never see him again.

* * *

Nor was I ever to see battle. Our operatives in those mills which had been converted to war production, utterly safe from any conceivable enemy action and enjoying wages many times the pay of our poor soldiers and sailors who faced death on tropical atolls and icy northern seas, chose this time to strike over the issue of unionization. My father, harassed by the negotiations, insulted by jeering picketers to whom he had paid the highest salaries in the industry and bitterly disillusioned by such blatant lack of patriotism, suffered a stroke which confined him to a wheelchair. Without consulting me, and much to my anguish, he instructed the War Department that I was the only person who could handle the emergency, and I found myself detached from active duty and "requested" by a vice admiral (no less!) to take over the management of the mills until further notice. That further notice never came, and I spent the rest of the war as a civilian. I was permitted to wear my uniform, but I was too disgusted to do so.

There have been those who attributed my firm and consistent postwar antilabor policy to my resentment of the operatives during the conflict and those who claimed I took advantage of my "war duty" to look into ways and means of ultimately moving some of the mills to states with poverty areas that might provide easier territory for my alleged "union busting." It is quite true that I was indignant with men who took advantage of a troubled time to improve (as they wrongly believed) their working conditions. It is even true that I despised their leaders. But at all times my mind was capable of seeing clearly enough what was best for the industry, the owners and the operatives. I think my subsequent career, however sneered at, has adequately proved that.

The news that Eric was killed on Guadalcanal came to me not only from the distance but as if from the past. My reaction was curiously numb. I thought of him at times in the evening, when I paused in reading aloud to my drowsy and rapidly failing father. The severance between Eric and me had now been confirmed. He had passed finally and heroically into a realm of romance in which he had never believed. I had been abandoned, just as finally indeed, to the prosaic world of business management.

But with, as it turned out, one saving grace. Or what I had certainly hoped would be a saving grace. Nancy, who had always loved my father and been loved by him — he had made no secret of his longing for our marriage — came up to Rhinebeck to attend his funeral shortly after V-J Day. Following the service, she and I went on a long ramble by the river. To my surprise and delight she did not abruptly change the subject when I mentioned, though as something inevitable, Father's disappointment that his hopes about us had not been fulfilled.

"Is what you're getting at that your father *and* my mother couldn't both have been wrong?"

"Something like that."

"What about your mother? Was she for it, too?"

"Oh, she'd accept anything I did."

"Because she doesn't really care?"

"Because she knows I'm a very practical fellow."

"Would it be practical to marry a girl who's wasted so much of her silly self on a lost cause? *She's* certainly not very practical."

"I have enough practicality for two."

"Maybe that's too much."

"And I don't believe for a minute there isn't plenty of your far from silly self left."

She turned to me now, very grave and oddly passionate. "Damn it all, I think you're right! I don't see any reason why I shouldn't be a good wife, a devoted wife, a loyal and helping wife. And damn it all again, I *want* to do something with my life! Why the hell shouldn't I?"

Our eyes met in a long, silent stare. "I warn

you, Nancy, I'm ready to take you on those terms."

She swung around and walked several steps away from me. Then she spoke without turning. "Why don't you go home now, Hugh? You ought to be with your mother this afternoon. I want to go on walking alone. You've given me too much thinking to do for us to be talking."

And then, of course, I knew I had her. Indeed, I jogged blithely all the way back. And the very next morning I received her note: "What is left of Miss Nancy Van Pelt, whether silly or not, accepts with great pleasure and only the mildest foreboding the kind invitation of the venturesome Mr. Hugh Hammersly."

4

Let me say right off that in the dozen years that elapsed before Nancy left me — under circumstances which, in the eyes of every friend and relative we had, totally justified her — she was true blue. She had undertaken to be a devoted and loyal wife, and she had proved herself more than that, a cheerful one, as well as a wonderful mother to our little Hughie and Lisa. I had never had any close friends after Eric, and she was both popular and naturally gregarious, yet she took pains in our social life to cultivate the people who were least apt to dislike me. She spread over all her activities, both home and abroad, the fine silk covering of her bubbling laughter.

It was odd that we never seemed to quarrel. Sometimes I thought it very odd.

Father had left me both the house in town and the place in Rhinebeck, as well as making me trustee of his residuary estate, so I was in essential control of the family destinies. I gave the use of the town house to my mother and sister (the latter had preferred good works to marriage) and bought a large Park Avenue co-op for Nancy and me. Rhinebeck I reserved for the joint use of all of us in summers and on weekends. And how did Nancy cope with sharing a house, even part of the year, with a none-too-easy mother-in-law? I couldn't fault her. If she minded, you'd never have guessed it. Mother doted on her. I once congratulated Nancy on handling so well what was generally considered a difficult relationship.

"Would you rather your mother and I fought over you?" she asked keenly.

"Well, it might be nice to feel you weren't

both *quite* so content to let the other have her full share of me."

"Really, Hugh! Have I ever let you down in anything you really cared about?"

"Never!"

"Then stop complaining!" But, perhaps seeing that I was genuinely if unreasonably troubled, she added, "You know there are no people in the world I care more about than you and Hughie and Lisa."

None in this world. But there was someone who was no longer in this world. Was I becoming like the duke in "My Last Duchess"? Did I resent the fact that Nancy's smiles went everywhere? Did I want them all for myself? Selfish monster, I was jealous of a ghost, and there is no cure for that.

"What a piece of work is man!" Hamlet exclaims. "How noble in reason! How excellent in faculties!" But in none more than man's ingenuity in making hash out of what might have been a happy life. The only solution that I could see to my problem lay in burying myself in work. These years saw the doubling and tripling of the number of Hammersly mills. I expanded the list of our products, adding picture frames, plumbing fixtures, upholstery and all kinds of household gadgets. I made forays into other states where I could beat the unions by paying higher wages than in the mills they had organized, a device made possible by the greater profits engendered by my own system of unhampered work rules. I may have been widely hated, but my operatives were the most prosperous in the industry.

All of this involved my being away from home, visiting the different plants that I supervised, a goodly part of the year. Yet Nancy never complained. No, indeed, she never complained. But I was troubled by the ever widening gap between myself and her circle of friends.

Not, I hasten to add, that these were wide-eyed radicals. Some were even richer than I. Many had gone to private schools and were listed in the *Social Register*. But there was a kind of greatest common denominator in what I called the "party line" of their *New York Times* liberalism, a tolerant open-mindedness towards everything from buggery to Bolshevism. The majority were Democrats, though I suspect their fat purses made them secretly relieved at the increasing number of prominent millionaires in that party's leadership. What they really wanted was to have their cake of liberalism and eat it, too. Of course, they all disliked me thoroughly, but they didn't begin to show it openly until the rise of Joe McCarthy.

The Wisconsin senator, whose death was in the paper this very morning, did not yield quite the influence which the journalists, who created him, maintained. Some of their readers might find it hard to believe that the bravest thing a man could do, at the very height of his alleged reign of terror, was to stand up for him at a Park Avenue dinner party. I never approved of his sloppy habit of using gossip and at times even lies as the basis of his allegations, but I did, and still do, believe that the Communist Party had made dangerous inroads into our public and private institutions and that what he *aimed* to accomplish was entirely commendable. Yet in that excited time distinctions were lost. If you didn't want the senator hanged, drawn and quartered you were a fascist beast, and that was all there was to it.

As I have never condescended to restrain my tongue, the parties Nancy and I went to began to be marred by disagreeable altercations. It irritated me that Nancy herself, while obviously disagreeing with all my political principles, seemed to regard me as too hopelessly entrenched in my point of view to be worthy of debate. When I taxed her once with this, she simply retorted, "Well, aren't you?"

"Aren't *you?*"

"All right, let's agree we both are, and leave

it at that. These are not easy times for either of us. I think we'd much better declare a truce zone at home."

But our truce was soon to be broken, and it was I, alas, who broke it.

Nancy and I and Mother belonged to an ancient Manhattan discussion group which met after dinner on winter Wednesday evenings at members' homes large enough to cope with a hundred or more guests. A lecture by a professional expert on a current topic would be followed by a question-and-answer period, champagne and an elegant supper. One morning when I was away at our mill in Lowell, Nancy telephoned to remind me that the group was meeting the following night at my mother's.

"Does she want me to introduce the speaker?" I asked. "I can take an evening shuttle tomorrow."

"Actually not. That's not why I called. She and I both think you'd be happier *not* being there."

"Why? Have you got some kind of commie speaking?"

"One who *you* may think is that. Chester Dobel."

I breathed hard. "Well, I won't introduce him, that's for sure. But I still think I'd better be on hand. My presence may keep him from leading you all in 'The International.' "

"Oh, Hugh dear, *promise* me you won't make a scene!"

"Good-bye, my sweet," I said firmly. "Don't expect me for dinner. I'll dress here and go straight from the plane to Mother's."

Chester Dobel was my particular *bête-noire*. He had gone to Harvard with a number of Nancy's friends and made a name for himself as a campus radical, even resigning from his club there with a public and priggish denunciation of its admissions policy. In the war he had attracted wide attention by declaring that he would serve only if enrolled in a Negro regiment, and if he had not been a card-carrying communist, he was the most loyal of fellow travellers. More recently he had trimmed his liberal sails to the new anti-Stalinism of liberaldom and was giving dulcet lectures on how a benign socialism might provide a haven for disillusioned Reds. He was a small, plump creature with thick curly hair and ruby lips which I could swear were made up.

When I arrived, the lecture had already begun. I spotted Nancy in the front row, directly under the speaker, but I preferred to be with Mother, who was seated alone, rather imperially, in an alcove slightly raised above the main floor, swathed, as she always seemed to be, in white, with an ermine wrap about her neck to protect her from any draft. She might have been Gertrude in the play scene, and I was as mordant as Hamlet.

Gazing bleakly about at the audience, I felt that it might be mocking me. Enclosed in those high walls of linenfold paneling hung with dark tapestries of medieval hunts, under a ceiling carved with Tudor roses and drawbridges, that smug gathering of Manhattan's elected souls seemed to be proclaiming its smug dedication to the higher things of life. Did their number not include the banner members of many boards of museums, of orchestras, of libraries? If a sudden blaze had reduced the vast chamber to ashes, would the cultural life of the city survive? I glanced balefully at my mother, the poetess, her eyes half-closed, dreaming no doubt of another ode. Fit priestess for such an assembly!

And who was the toad that squatted beside her on the dais but the crude maker of vulgar household objects, the slave driver, the philistine, the soul of corporate greed! For *that* was how they all saw me, *me,* who had had in my heart more poetry, more vision of beauty, than any of them had even dreamed of! And if the world of dreary fact had closed over that vision, if a chill night had darkened my aspirations, at least I knew it! And *faced* it!

I forced myself now to attend the unctuous tones of the loathsome Dobel. His small indulgent smile, hovering at the edges of his cherubic lips, seemed to encourage his listeners to rise to the liberal goals he pointed to in a cerulean sky. And now he was talking about the Stalin purges. Yes, he had actually the nerve to palliate them!

"That great wrongs were committed in those days, there seems to be no doubt. That many were doomed to an unjust death, I fear we must accept. Conceivably, the enemies of social progress may have exaggerated the number, but even a single wrongful killing we must deplore. I, for one, have never been able even to accept the shooting of the Czar, much less that of his innocent family. But I impenitently insist that there was still a message of hope for humanity in the core of the Marxist doctrine and that we should not throw away the baby with the dirty bath water. It may take courage to say it in this year of our Lord 1956, but it is still a year of our Lord, and who has not spotted elements of communism in Christ's disdain of material things?"

Christ! What had he to do with Christ? Or myself, for that matter? I had never felt that Christian icons had much relation to my life. They might have had for Mother; they very likely had for Father; and certainly they had much to do with the dark shades and harsh sunlight of Chelton School. But I had had the oppressed sense of other deities, no less inexorable, awaiting me in the alleyways of sleep and daydreams, such as Shamash, Sun God of Suse, at whose high turban and straight beard descending in formal ringlets to his chest I had gazed in awe in Father's collection of Mideast statuary. He had seemed to fix his bulbous, beady, ebony eyes upon the boy Hugh to ordain him as his priest to create order where order there was none.

All I remember now was that I was suddenly on my feet, shouting, "I want no more of this blasphemous and treasonable talk in this house!"

There was a ghastly silence, followed by gasps of protest; and then Dobel asked, almost politely, "You wish to speak, Hugh? Well, why not? We needn't wait for the question period."

"Don't you call me Hugh. And I request you to leave this house at once!"

"Friends, friends!" I recall the rustle of Mother's robe as she rose beside me. "I'm afraid my son has taken leave of his senses. Please, please, be seated, all. Hugh and I will go into the library. And do go on with your talk, Mr. Dobel, I beg of you."

"No!" I cried.

"Hugh, must I remind you that you're in *my* house?"

"But it's not! It's mine. Do you want me to summon the police?"

The assembly looked to Mother in dismay and astonishment. And no doubt with some inner delight at such a wondrous scene.

"In that case, we'd better all leave," Mother announced superbly. "I shall certainly not spend another night under the same roof as you, Hugh Hammersly. You have disgraced our family. Nancy, dear, will you call the Colony Club to see if they have a room for me at this hour?"

"No, Ma-in-law." Nancy had risen and was coming down the aisle towards us. She swept me with a quick glance of contempt. "You'll come to me. *Hugh* can stay here. In *his* house."

When I called, in great contrition, at my apartment the next morning to beg Mother to return to the house, she received me in my own living room as if I were a guest on very strict probation. She informed me that she would never go back so long as I held the deed to her home; it would have to be transferred to her. I was not so overwhelmed with guilt as to refrain from pointing out that this would be folly tax-wise, and we compromised on a life estate for her, with remainder over to my issue and my sister. Poetesses, I found, can be very practical persons.

My interview (for that is what it was) with Nancy was less easy. She came into the room as soon as Mother left it, very direct and businesslike, not angry but firm.

"This is going to take some time, Hugh. Last night was a very bad shock. We must certainly separate for a while. Whether permanently or not I cannot tell now. If you want this apartment, I'll move right out. You needn't give me any money; you've already given me more than enough. And there'll be no trouble about the children. You can see them whenever and wherever you want. Of course, we'll have to keep in touch about many things. But time I must have."

"I can't blame you," I muttered. "I couldn't even blame you if you never loved me again."

"Well, you certainly weren't very lovable last night."

"It was a kind of madness. I don't know what came over me."

"That's what I've got to find out — just what *did* come over you."

"It's not, however, that I was wrong about your phony friend. He, at least . . ."

"Please, Hugh! Not again!"

There was nothing I could do but leave.

Of course I let her have the apartment, and I moved to my club.

For the rest of the winter and spring I travelled from mill to mill, steeping myself in work even more furiously than before, as if enlarging my fortune was the only way I could preserve my mental health or make up to my offspring whatever misfortune their father's eccentric behavior might have brought down on their innocent heads. But seeing nobody but obsequious subordinates and having lost in Nancy my anchor to any kind of real sanity, I became even more moody and introspective and increased the number of cocktails that I took before my lonely dinner from one to three or even four. My mind was filled with beastly images and my sleep horribly restless.

When summer came and Nancy informed me that she was taking the children to her brother in Maine and would not be using the big house on the Southampton dunes that I had rented because Hughie Junior had expressed a desire for an ocean as opposed to a river vacation, I decided that I did not want to be alone with Mother in Rhinebeck and that I would occupy the leased cottage by myself.

What happened there . . . but I need not go into *that* again. In the words that Thomas

Hardy used about his unhappy heroine Tess, I can only hope that the President of the Immortals has finished his sport with Hugh.

5

Nancy Hammersly, having finished reading her husband's manuscript in the waiting room of Dr. Burns's Park Avenue office, took her seat again before his desk. He had a long, thoughtful, wrinkled countenance and appropriately steel-grey hair.

"I think I should start by telling you, Doctor, that my old feeling for Eric Potter had long subsided. He was, of course, always a memory, sometimes a dear one, sometimes not. He was a very selfish and a very lazy man."

"And did you ever tell your husband that?"

"No. Curiously enough, I didn't believe he wanted to hear it. He liked to think of Eric as his romantic ideal. And of me as a part of all that."

Burns seemed to wonder. "Do you mean that the romance that he thought had gone out of his life might somehow survive in you and the memory of Eric?"

"Romanticism can be a tough weed."

"And a dangerous one. The leaders of the French Reign of Terror were raised on the pastoral dreams of Rousseau."

"You think Hugh would like to send us all to the guillotine?"

He smiled. "Only those who don't agree he has their best interests at heart."

"Must he be stuck with that forever? What's your prognosis, Doctor?"

"It depends on you. Are you willing to consider going back to him?"

"I think so."

"Do you still love him?"

"Not in the way I loved Eric, no. But I wouldn't want that now. Hugh's been a good husband and father. I'm hoping this experience may teach him that he's like other humans. Just as pathetic. And just as disgusting."

"But he's not disgusting to you?"

"No. But you know what I mean."

"And can you forgive him?"

"The calls to those girls? Oh, yes." She smiled. "Actually, they give me something to build on. I prefer the little boy talking smut on the telephone to the warrior who defends me from Reds."

"To My Beloved Wife . . ."

1

There are times in the lives of some people which they tend to regard as more "real" than others, and for Lucy Cross, facing the climacteric of her sixtieth birthday in 1934, there was no question but that the 1880s, or at least the 1880s of central Virginia, had been that time. For there had to be a greater reality in the genteel poverty of the Dales, of *her* Dales, anyway, than in the limitless resources of the New York Crosses. Reality for Lucy had been the tumbledown manor house in Albemarle County, the scraggy remnant of the once broad plantation maintained by two old "darkies," former slaves, underpaid but ignorantly loyal, and the bickering of her always ailing mother and alcoholic father, pale survivors of an Old Dominion clan. She had never, even after thirty-five years of marriage, been wholly able to believe in the pot of gold from which the rainbow of her family-in-law seemed to ascend.

The coming of the Depression, with its long breadlines and defenestration of brokers, had seemed to bring New York closer to her childhood, though its effect on her husband had been minimal. Indeed, Ezra Cross's loss of half his great fortune had only made him more grossly wealthy in the disgruntled eyes of the many who had lost three quarters, or all, of their own. Was there one servant the less to maintain, in stately, perfect order, the long succession of chambers in the Park Avenue triplex filled with priceless Americana? Had not the curator (for Ezra had his own) only the day before stipulated that the giant dresser in Ezra's bedroom be banished to storage, recent research having established its origin as Dutch and not from the the Manhattan workshop of Duncan Phyfe? Life went on, pretty much as usual.

But at least the friends who came to the apartment now talked "poor," though they would always, at times rudely, deny to Lucy the least possibility of sharing their new and perhaps even interesting state, making such remarks as: "Of course, you, my dear, will never have to worry about such mundane matters," or, "There'd have to be an interplanetary collision before *you'd* ever feel the pinch." But Lucy did not feel guilty, as they obviously wished her to feel, because she had never regarded herself as rich. The *Crosses* were rich, and, God knew, Ezra felt guilty enough about it, or at least he *had,* in the early days of their marriage, when he had tried to substitute in the public mind for every malefaction of his ruthless father a monumental charitable grant. But although she had been at all times intimately associated with the philanthropy which they had, between them, turned into a kind of business, or at least a life occupation, and although she had been widely credited in the press with having been as much her husband's guide as his helpmate, she had never received anything more than an adequate household allowance from him. It was the same with the children. He wrote any reasonable check they requested, but he kept the checkbook. His money was to him a sacred trust. Nor had she minded. At least until lately. Because it had seemed to maintain her "reality."

But now she had begun to think that she wanted to go into quite other fields of charitable endeavor than the ones on which she and Ezra had hitherto agreed: hospitals, medical and nursing schools and medical research. The Depression was undermining all hitherto established values, and Lucy found herself swept along in the current of the New Deal with an enthusiasm which had startled her quite as much as it had her family. Her daughter, Evie, had baldly told her that she attributed her vote for Roosevelt to a delayed menopause. Her sons, Jimmy and Danny, were not so rude, but it was evident that they believed there was some kind of psychic explanation for so drastic a deviation from the Cross philosophy.

Ezra, always moderate, always kind, simply waited for this new phase in an adored spouse to spend itself. His own beliefs, anchored to his Presbyterian faith, were strong and fixed. He held that there were two fundamental forces in a democratic society: one, the force of the capitalist pioneer such as his father, and the other, that of his philanthropic son and heir. On these two principles hung all the economic law and its profits. Each was necessary; each divinely balanced the other to maintain freedom and prosperity.

It worried Lucy that her change of heart and mind had come so fast and so inexorably. Had she been waiting all these years for the moment when the leak should appear in the hitherto impregnable Cross dike? In the past she had scoffed at her cynical brother Tom, who maintained, despite his own complete dependence on his brother-in-law, that the time always came, in the life of every American heir to a great fortune, when he would succumb at last to the belief that he had somehow earned the money himself. Had that happened to Ezra? Had the money so seeped into his soul that he identified it with his own virtue? Had it happened to her children? Already?

This new, upsetting and yet exhilarating sea change in Lucy's outlook on life had not been purely political. A popular old bachelor and diner-out, Caspar Goodwillie, had aroused her interest in a new magazine which he and a group of literary-minded friends had recently founded. It was called *Castalia*, and it was dedicated to the promotion of such *avant-garde* poetry and fiction as would find scant welcome in the popular periodicals. Lucy, who was a lifetime reader of the English classics and who tended, like most of her friends and all of her relations, to look askance at free verse and at novels of what Ezra called "radical or pornographic tendencies," found herself catapulted into a new and entrancing world. But she had enough insight into her own psychology to recognize that the rapidity of her conversion was apt to indicate that a reaction against the Cross philosophy of life must have been brewing for a long time within her.

"You haven't even read Joyce!" Caspar exclaimed with raised hands. "What a joy to find so keen a mind virgin to such delights! It will be a rare privilege, my dear Lucy, if you will allow me to act as your humble guide."

"As my guide, anyway," she corrected him, smiling.

She read *Ulysses* and dipped deeply into Eliot, Pound, Gide and Proust. She found that she could now face boldly enough the evident fact that what had initially attracted her to this new mentor was Ezra's dislike and distrust of him. Caspar was soft and pale and fat, with a round face topped by snowy hair and rendered serious by beady dark eyes, which seemed to snap with intelligence. He dressed with excessive elegance and was not in the least ashamed of his fussy effeminate manners, balancing them with sudden eruptions of a terrible temper that made his features stern and his voice almost stentorian. He was rich, though not remotely like Ezra, and he lived in an exquisite Japanese house, the upper stories of which contained his great collection of twentieth-century manuscripts and first editions. He was also a snob, except with handsome young male poets, and Lucy was perfectly aware of his designs on the Cross Foundation for grants to his protégés, but so long as he professed to find her "a pearl among swine," as he did not scruple to put it, she was willing to accept his commendations as only three-quarters flattery. She had come to depend on him, in a matter of only months, for her principal amusement in life.

Her new interest did not pass unnoticed by her family. "Ma's Marxist rag," as *Castalia* was promptly dubbed by her children, was the butt of constant jibes. Not, however, by Ezra, who maintained an ominous silence about it. It was never his way to speak of a matter until he had done his "homework," and she knew well enough that he would not lightly dismiss her concern for a magazine which had already caused her to skip two board meetings of his foundation and several grant conferences.

The inevitable crisis came on the night of her birthday, celebrated as always by a dinner party at home limited to the immediate family. Looking over the head of her husband, sitting opposite her at the huge portrait of herself by Lazlo, she decided that for once she might at least act the woman he had tried to paint. For like all the subjects of that fashionable artist, her image was amost impossibly aristocratic. The sweeping scarlet evening gown, the long, pale, bare, elegant arms and exposed ivory neck and shoulders, the high fine brow and cheekbones, the haughty gaze of the brooding dark eyes, the smooth raven hair with here and there a speck of white seemed to evoke some Austrian archduchess who had silently stooped to wed a Balkan monarch. It was the way Ezra liked to see her. Well, now perhaps he would! There was no likeness of *him* anywhere in the vast apartment, but then he owned the apartment and everything in it. Everything inorganic, anyway.

She dropped her eyes to return her husband's gaze. His was full of the quiet benignity which suited the straight, trim figure, still youthful at seventy, and the long, lineless, pale face under the stiff, grizzled hair. Ezra struck her that night as trying, almost wistfully, to look less dry. Had all the guilt and neuroses of his younger years hardened into that fine glaze of serenity? Yet he was a good man. His gaze appealed to her with love and fidelity, only one of which she had been able fully to return.

Jimmy, on her right, seemed to have waxed even blander and blonder now that he had passed his thirty-third year. He was handsome, certainly, but not interestingly so, and his mild blue eyes seemed perpetually engaged in the genial effort to persuade one that he took in both sides of questions of which one knew he saw only one. On his father's right sat Faith, his wife, small and brown and mechanically smiling, never perhaps admitting even to herself how much the Crosses bored her.

Evie, husbandless for the moment, on her father's left, now losing her buxom blond prettiness to added flesh, manifested her intense self-absorption by habitual mannerisms, raising a finger to touch her hair, twisting a shoulder, arching her neck, focusing her eyes on a questioner with an obvious effort to escape momentarily from some engrossing fantasy. Like many of her generation of heiresses, she had demonstrated her independence solely by marrying men her father disliked.

And Danny, his mother's favorite, on her left, still a bachelor, short, black-haired, grinning, possessed of a sometimes cruel wit, seemed, for all his aggressiveness, to be fighting a losing battle with his father's quiet, patient and ineluctable determination to bring his sons into line with his philanthropic tradition.

They had reached the point in the birthday feast when it was traditional for Ezra to offer Lucy her "big" present. He tapped gently on his glass — his water glass. No wine or spirits had been served at any table of his since the passage of the Eighteenth Amendment, and he had chosen to continue this "wholesome abstention" after its recent repeal. The butler and waitress discreetly withdrew.

"The time has come, my children, to ask your dear mother for what worthy cause or causes, or to satisfy what personal wish of her own, she would like me to draw her birthday check. We know that she usually tends to favor a charity that she deems insufficiently recognized by our foundation in the preceding year, but on this special birthday, if she were to select something for herself alone — even some lovely ornament of personal adornment — I think we should all be gratified."

Lucy's mind reflected the sudden image of herself looking out a window on the first day of spring and seeing only signs of a late snow in the clouds above. Then the picture changed. Was it King Lear, facing her down the table, complacently awaiting the expected tribute of expressed love? Suppose she were to ask him for a diamond tiara? She had seen one, only the day before, in the window of Tiffany's, reputedly once worn by the Empress Josephine. Oh, he would buy it for her, yes. But how quickly the benevolence would fade from those glassy eyes!

"Oh, I'm sure Ma's going to ask for a new common room for the Lucy Cross Nursing School," Evie interjected, a yawn in her tone. "Or something like that. But I agree with you, Pa. I wish she'd be selfish for once. How about a little jewel of a palazzo on the Grand Canal? Just a tiny one, of course."

Danny snickered. "So you could borrow it for your honeymoon with Ben Sneed? That is, if you can ever persuade him to quit the beach he's combing in Jamaica for the Lido."

Evie, used to him, shrugged. "You're too cheap to be borne."

"Children, children!" Ezra reproached them. "Please remember this is your mother's day. Let us all love one another." Then he smiled, to indicate that his qualification was only a joke. "Or at least pretend we do."

Jimmy, always ready to bring in the family mission when his father was present, sought now to elevate the tone. "I wonder if Mother might not be interested in a literary project. We all know of her enthusiasm for her new magazine." He glanced at his father with the slightest of nods and smiles, as if to signify their joint recognition of a mild, a perhaps even amiable weakness in an otherwise stalwart soul. He then turned to his mother. "What would you say, Ma, to extending your patronage to a research project? There's a professor of economics at Berkeley called Hobbs who's applied to the foundation for a grant supporting his preparation of a biography of Grandpa Cross. He's taking what strikes me as a new and interesting line. He claims that Grandpa's stock market operations were not the isolated, unrelated speculations that have long been supposed, but were actually coordinated to control prices, to curb inflation and to introduce a kind of order to the sale and purchase of securities."

"In short, that the 'wolf of Wall Street' was really a sheep in wolf's clothing?" asked Danny.

Lucy glanced curiously from the grinning Danny to his father. The latter looked cautiously amused. Evidently his younger son had romped perilously close but not quite over the permitted boundaries. Some liberty, she supposed, had to be accorded to the young seals in their training. Danny could occasionally drop his rubber ball and still receive the tossed fish. She sighed, but it was a sigh of irritation. Would *she,* after all, have to do the leading?

"What do *you* think of this Hobbs project, Ezra?" she asked seriously.

"Well, it may seem a bit farfetched," he replied with a little cough. "But it *is,* as Jimmy says, an interesting idea. I have always felt that my father was basically a misunderstood man. And although I'm not entirely convinced that Professor Hobbs can prove as much coordination in Father's many ventures as he claims, I have always suspected a certain civic consciousness somewhere at the root of his operations."

And even if Ezra *knew* that was utter rot, Lucy reflected, as he must, deep down, unless he had packed his cellar of truth too tightly with fatuity, he would be happy to publish this silly book as the epiphany of the god of the Crosses. Mysterious indeed were the ways of that deity!

"Do you suggest, then, Ezra, that underwriting this biography might be a worthy use of my birthday money?"

"Well, only if you agreed, my dear. I want only what you want."

"I hope that will still be so when I tell you what I *do* want."

Ten expectant eyes turned to her.

"What I should really like," she now stated in a firm, clear tone, "would be to do something significant for *Castalia*. I believe that America today is bursting with new literary talent. I believe we should foster it. It needs much more than a magazine. It needs a publishing house. I should like a gift, if you will be so generous, Ezra, that will mark an important first step in establishing a house dedicated to supporting the kind of innovative literature which cannot, at least at this point, command a wide reading public. My friend Caspar Goodwillie assures me that if we can lead the way, he can round up enough financial support to make a solid board."

She had not taken her eyes off her husband. His countenance expressed no surprise. Was there nothing he failed to anticipate? Jimmy stared down at his plate. Danny for once did not grin. Even Evie ceased to be bored.

"But, Ma, isn't *Castalia* as Red as that dress in your portrait?"

Jimmy was more moderate than his sister. "I must admit that one of our leading investment bankers expressed surprise to me the other day that Mother should allow her name to be on the masthead."

Lucy looked to Danny. What would *he* say? He started well enough. "Oh, I think *Castalia*'s all right. I think it's fine, really. We need an organ for the left, if only to keep it from bursting." But then he went on. "A publishing house, though. Isn't that going rather far?"

And now thus spaketh Ezra: "I confess to a personal objection to your mother's project. She and I have worked together so long and so closely in the vineyard of public service that I cannot but deplore the idea of supporting a scheme which will enlist her efforts alone."

"But why can't we work on it together, Ezra?"

"Because, my dear, I cannot reconcile the support of so radical a periodical, much less a publishing house, with my principles. I took the occasion recently to read an issue of *Castalia* from cover to cover. There were two poems in free verse — which to my benighted eyes is no verse at all — that described the act of human reproduction (which I believe should be left to books on biology and medicine) in terms that I can only describe as lewd. And there was a eulogy of Mr. Roosevelt's New Deal which criticized it only in falling short of the Russian Five-Year Plan. But worst of all was the first chapter of a novel to be serialized in later issues which dealt with the problems of the red Indian today in terms which implied that the whites were the real savages."

Danny pounced on this. "That's all because of Ma's descent from Pocahontas!"

"My great-great-grandmother Dale, Danny, was *not* descended from Pocahontas, as you well know," Lucy retorted with some heat. "She was a simple Algonkin squaw. Which gives me, admittedly, an interest in undoubted Indian wrongs. But that is only a small part of my interest in *Castalia.* Of course angry and talented young writers are going to go to extremes. Of course they are going to use extravagant and sometimes coarse language. Some will even be communists. But I believe very strongly that they should be heard."

"But, Lucy dearest, are you quite sure that *Castalia* isn't already a communist organ? Are you sure the real editor isn't in Moscow?"

"I *am* sure. But I'm not a bit sure that he won't be if I and Caspar lose control!"

"Oh, Ma!"

"Really, Mother, I've never heard you so passionate."

"Maybe it's an improvement."

Lucy at this last smiled at Danny.

But Ezra held up a hand. "Well, my dear, I see this discussion is futile. Let us not raise our voices. For your gift I am happy to draw you a check for five thousand dollars. For anything you choose. And no questions asked!"

2

Lucy's branch of the Virginia Dales had a peculiar genealogical twist of which they had once been ashamed, but of which, in later years, the more enlightened had been inclined to boast. A Dale boy in the eighteenth century had been kidnapped by Algonkins in the western part of the state and brought up by the tribe. He had wedded a squaw, and their son had grown up to be a chief. Captured by frontiersmen, this young leader had been recognized and reclaimed by his father's kin; he had married a Dale cousin and become Lucy's great-grandfather. Thus the Dales, in the direct male line, had gone from white to red and back to white again.

Lucy had always been proud of the high cheekbones and of the peculiarly alabaster skin which she was supposed to owe to the mixing of blood strains. But in recent years she had taken a more serious interest in the story of the ancestral tribe, which was, as Danny had gleaned, the reason for her sponsorship of the novel to which Ezra referred. It had become her fantasy to conceive of herself as separated by the barrier of race from her human milieu — not simply from friends and acquaintances, but from her husband and children as well. It had pleased her to cultivate the image of a proud and defiant squaw, brought home a captive from a noble wilderness to a settlement of smugly complacent colonists who saw in the brave forests which carpeted the New World only pulp for paper on which to record the banality of their own annals. And her soul would always yearn to retrieve that lost Eden.

Caspar Goodwillie's beady eyes swelled on the morning after her birthday, when, in the small but neatly appointed office of *Castalia* on Lafayette Street, she told him of the amount of her gift.

"Of course, I don't mean to sniff at five

grand," he remarked, after a moment's reflection. "But may I hope its the herald of a more princely donation?"

"I'm afraid not. Ezra disapproves of all literature that couldn't appear in *The Saturday Evening Post*. And once he makes up his mind, he never changes it. His credo is consistency."

"Then our publishing house is *finito*."

"Why? Is Ezra the only millionaire in the world?"

"There are others, true. And others I could approach. But it would involve a complete change of plans. I'd have to find another big name as a starter. What I really mean, my dear Lucy, is that it will be *finito* as far as *your* participation in the project is concerned."

"How can that be?"

"Can you ask? My good friend, consider the facts. We're faced with having to raise something like half a million bucks. So I approach my first victim. His first question, after looking at the names on my proposed board, will be: 'How much is Mrs. Cross pledging?' When he hears five *g*'s he will tell me to write him down for that sum. Nobody, Lucy, will give *more* than Mrs. Ezra Cross. It would be impossible to have you on the board with a commitment of less than fifty thousand."

"I see," she mused. "I *do* see."

"Can't you put up that much on your own?

Without even asking Ezra?"

She shook her head sadly. "He owns everything. He pays all the bills. Oh, I suppose I could sell my jewelry. Except it wouldn't bring that much. I've never really cared for jewelry."

"I know! The proud, plainly adorned Indian chieftess."

"Caspar, you're a fiend," she murmured, blushing.

"Of course, you can go on with *Castalia.* Five thou is a good gift for *it.* I can get it matched half a dozen times over. But will you do this for me? Will you give a dinner party for my prospective donors?"

"Of course."

"And do you think you could possibly persuade Ezra to let some liquor be served? If *I* supply it?"

"I doubt it."

"Ah, well, a bid from Mrs. Ezra Cross will probably do the trick, even without the hooch. I'll warn them to tank up before they come."

Lucy that night, dining alone with Ezra, decided to make one more appeal. He listened to her gravely, but his eyes remained cast down at the table surface. At her first pause he remarked dolefully, "If you *knew* how painful this was to me, dearest, I do not think you'd put me through it."

"Painful to *you,*" she retorted indignantly. "Ezra, I'm trying to tell you what this whole thing means to *me.* To me, your wife, your helpmate, as you've always liked to call me. I'm not asking you to *approve* of this project. I'm asking you to do it as a favor. Because it's something dear to me, something close to my heart."

"Lucy, darling, this is killing me!"

"If *I* had the money, I'd give it to you for anything you wanted!"

"Even something you morally disapproved of?"

"Certainly! Though it's hard to imagine your wanting anything I'd morally disapprove of."

"Supposing I wanted the money for some foreign act of terrorism? Say, an assassination?"

"Now you're being ridiculous. Anyway, you ought to trust my judgment. I wouldn't be asking money for anything like that."

"But you don't know all the people you'd be supporting. I have to stand by my principles, Lucy!"

"Which you prefer to your wife. And you call that love?"

" 'I could not love thee, dear, so much . . .' "

" 'Loved I not honor more,' " she finished for him tartly. "No woman has ever called *that* love."

Ezra at last raised his eyes to confront hers. She was startled but not moved by the pain in them. "Isn't there something else I can do for you, Lucy?"

"Yes! You can let me serve cocktails and wine at a dinner party I'm planning."

"A party for whom?"

"Never mind!"

"But you know my principles about intoxicating beverages."

"Damn your principles! I'm going to order the drinks I want for my party, and if you choose to stop my serving them, you'll have to call a policeman!"

Ezra rose, deathly pale. "If you don't mind, my dear, I think I'll retire to my study. I'm feeling a bit ill." He started towards the door but turned back before reaching it. "Of course, you may serve anything you like at your party. But I assume you will not expect me to attend."

3

Lucy in the week that followed was appalled to find that her feeling for Ezra had turned into something she could only call dislike. She hardly spoke to him now, and when their paths crossed in the apartment she would respond to his invariable glance of mute appeal with a shrug or a toss of her head. She arranged to be out for lunch and saw to it that there were always guests for dinner. Once, when he cried out, "How long must you put me through this?" she answered that she did not know yet, that he had to give her time to think things out.

Lying in bed in the early morning she would review her early life to determine just how she had arrived where she was and why. It was perfectly clear to her that the misery of her premarital state had been absolute: the foreclosure of the plantation, the squeezing of the family into a squalid flat in Charlottesville, her father's fits of delirium tremens, her mother's slow and agonizing death of colon cancer. Where indeed, in what black hole might they not have ended up, had not a thirty-year-old bachelor, who just happened to be the only child and sole heir of the notorious Philemon Cross, purchased the Dale plantation and refurbished it until, like Cleopatra's barge, it "burnt on the water"?

This, of course, would not in itself have rescued the Dales; that had been accomplished by Ezra's conscience. Although he had only acquired the place from the Dales' foreclosing mortgagee, he deemed himself somehow their disinheritor. He sought them out and learned of their troubles; he paid the hospital expenses of Lucy's mother's last months and the charges of her father's sanitorium. He put her two brothers (including the sardonic Tom) through the University of Virginia and placed her retarded sister in an appropriate home. He even repurchased as many of the sold and scattered Dale heirlooms as could be traced and deeded them to the family, borrowing them back to adorn the manor house only so long as he should occupy it. And he asked Lucy to marry him.

It was thus perhaps not surprising that she, though not in the least in love with him, should have immediately accepted his proposal. He was not only the wondrous benefactor, the *deus ex machina* of the Dale destinies; he was a shy, graceful, modest, reticent man who couldn't believe that a young woman as pretty as Lucy could love him without the added inducement of gratitude. And although she could never imagine feeling for him anything like what she had felt for a handsome Virginia medical student who had found her family too hopeless a stumbling block, she saw perfectly, from the beginning, that Ezra was the type of man who had a greater need to love than to be loved, that she was faced with a unique opportunity for a rich and rewarding life with no cost to her conscience. For she might actually be able to give this good man *more* than he would be able to give her!

And hadn't she? Oh, yes, she had received a lot — yes — no one knew that better than she. She had snuggled down, from her first day of marriage, in the warm bliss of this unbelievable security, happily turning over the precious pillows of assured comfort, luxuriating in an existence where everything was and always would be paid for. She was not one of those who become easily accustomed to riches; her want had been too long and too keen. But that was only a state of mind, not a state of being. The latter in her case was always active. The honeymoon was hardly over before she began her self-assigned job of persuading Ezra that hiding away in Virginia was no way to avoid the stigma of his father's reputation, that he must go back to New York and build a name as famous as the paternal one but for an opposite reason.

The father had died only a year before their marriage, leaving the fortune to Ezra outright, and his first reaction had been to turn his back on it, to let the income, except for the relatively small portion needed for his living expenses, be distributed by a charitable trust over which he exercised little control. He could see no way, he confessed to Lucy, to enter his father's name in the category of those he called "contributing pioneers," men who had helped build the American economy. There was no great railroad or shipping line that he could point to, no invention or emporium or even humble household product. It was only too clear that Philemon had been simply a raider, a cornerer, a surpassing genius in those stock market maneuvers which lure gullible investors to their doom as surely as the Hamelin rats were led to theirs by the Pied Piper.

And it was *she* who shook Ezra by the shoulders and faced him about to embark on the career of philanthropy which made his name famous throughout the land! It was she who induced him to take over the management of his charitable trust and pour out not only the income of his fortune but the greater part of the principal to support medical education and research, concentrating in one field initially for greater effect, though in time expanding into areas of more general education and scholarship. And this was how he repaid her for thirty-five years of devoted partnership!

4

At the Colony Restaurant, at Caspar Goodwillie's permanently reserved table for lunch, she and her host sat alone. She had told him as soon as she came in that she wanted caviar and champagne, and both had been promptly supplied.

"What are you celebrating, Lucy?"

"The exorcism of a ghost. Perhaps a whole gallery of them. Anyway, you shall have all the liquor you want at the *Castalia* dinner."

"Good heavens. You brought Ezra around? What a prize!"

"A booby prize. It was all I got."

"He was adamant about the grant?"

"He was. Even though I gave it to him, hot and heavy."

Caspar eyed her curiously. "You had a real row?"

"Oh, a row." She shrugged. "Ezra doesn't row. He just looks hurt. But we hardly speak now."

"How long has *that* been going on?"

"For a couple of weeks. Since I last saw you."

Caspar eyed her refilled champagne glass. She could see in his eyes the glitter of a tiny hope that he might be actually on the threshold of world-shaking scandal. Could it be . . . ? She knew that he kept a treasured file of Manhattan anecdotes and tales that was supposed to go back forty years.

"Lucy, this isn't . . . *serious?*"

She looked at him with a quizzical smile. "You mean, would I leave Ezra? What would he do if I did?"

"He'd crumble to pieces! He'd give you everything he had for anything you want. Oh, Lucy, *do* try it! If only as a threat."

"You really think it would work?"

"The world would be yours!" Caspar threw up his fat hands in excitement. "Think of Ezra faced with the prospect of losing his Lucy! It would be unimaginable. We'd have our publishing company. Any number of them. We could expand into the world of music and opera. Oh, my dear, just think of the things you and I could do. It would be a New York renaissance!"

"But built on the wreck of my marriage. Whether or not Ezra gave in, he and I would never be the same."

"On the contrary, it would be a better marriage! Reconstituted on a more civilized basis."

She sipped her champagne and allowed him, all during their meal, to chatter on about the arts they would sponsor and to fantasize about the new fields they would explore. By the time he got to the lost cities he would excavate in Guatemala and the buried Atlantis he would dig up at the bottom of the Caribbean, she decided it was time to go home.

At the house she telephoned to Danny and asked him to stop by for a drink after work at the foundation.

"Did you say a *drink?*" he demanded. "Shall we meet at a bar, then? Or at your club?"

"No, I'm serving drinks in my sitting room now. In fact, I may mix myself one this very moment."

"Mother!"

"You'd better come round if you want to keep me sober."

He was there in half an hour. He looked curiously at the cocktail things on the little bar she had installed and then went over to mix himself a drink.

"For you?" he asked, turning to her with visible constraint.

"No, dear. I just wanted you to see of what I'm now capable." And when he was seated she told him about her chat with Caspar. "Of course, it was all a joke," she ended flatly.

"Of course it was no such thing."

"You mean, you think I'd actually leave your father?"

"Oh, no. You could never do that. But it concerns me that you evidently like to dream about it."

"What makes you so sure it's only a dream?"

"Because you know it would kill him. The mere threat would do that. You'd never even get to discussing terms."

She had a fantasy of two stout, black-gloved hands suddenly gripping her shoulders and forcing her down, down. "But *why*, if he loves me as he says he does, will he do *nothing* for what I care about?" Her appeal rose almost to a wail.

"Because he's taken it into his head that you're supporting something that undermines the capitalist system."

"The system that produced his hideous father!"

"And the one that produced *him*."

"What you're telling me, Danny, is that your father is as great an egotist as your grandfather ever was!"

"Greater! Because he's so goddamn *noble!* Face it, Ma. You're stuck. But don't despair. You're ten years younger than Dad, and women live longer than men, anyway. I'm not wishing him anything but a long and happy life. But the day may come when you'll have it all to yourself. To do with as you wish!"

"Never! He's been warned now. He'll put everything in a sacred trust."

She sighed deeply as she abandoned her dream. Danny was quite right. A dream was all it had been. But she had desperately wanted to live it.

A Day and Then a Night

1

Ted Atwood had never believed that he was as favored by the gods as he appeared to be. To have believed it would be a kind of *hubris,* would it not? Yet even his not believing it would not have placated them had they already decided on his fall. And *hubris* was not always a necessary preliminary; Oedipus had shown none. Other people might find him favored by the gods, but the gods didn't care about that. People found him sympathetic, responsive, even at times charming, but that was the easy trick of curly blond hair, blue eyes, a tight build and the habit of smiles. It seemed to him that their compliments built up a debt that he might not be able to pay, that it was no sure blessing to be adored by one's mother and stepfather, to be a favorite at the Bar Harbor Swimming Club, or even to be the chosen assistant of the great Professor Musgrave.

As he sat alone on a bright summer Maine morning on a rock at the peak of Cadillac Mountain, surveying the great grey placid spread of the Atlantic and the long green stretch of the distant mainland coast and then gazing down to where, more directly below him, more intimately, lay the colorful cubes of the village shopping district and beyond them the dark roofs, poking out over trees, of the shingle cottages of the summer folk, he felt as if he were being offered the kingdoms of the earth. But on one condition. That he refuse them. Because they weren't and couldn't ever be his.

Harvard had been his and was now behind him, as were the halcyon years of obtaining his master's in English lit. And he was due, after a summer of lounging at his family's summer retreat, to start joyously in New Haven as the assistant to Professor Musgrave in his famous course on the Jacobean dramatists. But none of this was really *true.* What was true and only true was the war.

He had always known it would come. That was an odd but important factor in his life. Ever since he could first remember things, in the years immediately following the Armistice, he had suffered from the conviction that his generation, like his father's, had a date with the trenches, and his recurrent nightmare had been of going "over the top," leaving the mud and rats and rain for darkness and bayonets and shells. How else could one become a man? It was as sure as puberty or boarding school or football or a twenty-first birthday party. But when he found, as he grew older, that his conviction was not shared by other boys, he learned to be silent about it. Perhaps it was not their fate but only his. And it was just a fate, too, not a test. He was not necessarily to be assessed for cowardice or bravery. The fighting might be too confused, the atmosphere too dark for that. It was even possible that he was simply to be killed. Like his father, at Château Thierry. For he never had any dreams of coming home.

Annette Simpson's dark head appeared over a ledge below. She looked up and waved to him. Her cheeks were as white and puffy as one of the few clouds on that peerless afternoon; her eyes black and nervously seeking — what? — and the spindly legs which supported her slender body moved unsurely over the rocks despite new and spotless sneakers. She had been driven to the peak on the new park road by her family's chauffeur; she had agreed to walk down the mountain with him but not up. It was like her.

Sitting beside him now, she took in the view and then put on her sunglasses.

"It's quite something, isn't it?"

She shrugged. "Well, of course, the island's full of views. I tend to confuse them with the postcards and picture cushions stuffed with pine needles and labeled 'Vacationland.' And now, of course, they're *passé.*"

"When does a view become *passé?*"

"When it doesn't tell the truth. Look at that ocean. What is the message it's trying to convey? Obviously one of peace. Eternal peace. Yet right out there. Or there. Or there" — she seemed to be jabbing her forefinger into the limitless grey-blue — "may lurk a U-boat."

His gaze was speculative. "Possibly. Though what it would be hunting up here is hard to imagine. It might be fun to put a torpedo through Atwater Kent's yacht in the cocktail hour. But he *is* a neutral."

"Well, he won't be for long. We're bound to get into it now, don't you think, Ted?"

"Not if my ma has anything to do with it."

"Oh, she'll have to give up that old America First business. Everyone up here sings Churchill's praises."

"Ma has never been ruled by 'everyone.' "

"But you don't go along with her, do you?"

He shook his head. "It's hard to say. I don't go along with her for *me.* But I'm not a hundred percent convinced that I mightn't if I wasn't me."

"Now what the hell do you mean by that?"

"Well, *I'm* going to get into it, that's for sure."

"You mean because you're so anti-Hitler?"

"Well, of course, we're all that. But is it really necessary, to know you're going to get into it?"

"Oh, I see. It's because your father was killed in the last war."

"That may be in it, of course. That I shan't be spared because he wasn't. That it wouldn't be fair. But it's really more of a sense of inevitability. I think I can best explain it by a poem that was found scribbled in a copy of *A Shropshire Lad* that belonged to a young Englishman who died in the trenches. His name was Patrick Shaw-Stewart. Shall I recite it to you?"

"All of it? Is it long?"

"I'll cut it to four stanzas. He was on leave in the Mediterranean after the Dardanelles campaign, but he was under orders to proceed to Flanders." Ted paused. He recalled that this poem, when he recited it to himself, would bring tears to his eyes. This mustn't happen before Annette. But it wouldn't. He made his voice impersonal.

> "But other shells are waiting
> Across the Aegean sea,

Shrapnel and high explosive,
Shells and hells for me.

Achilles came to Troyland
And I to Chersonese:
He turned from wrath to battle
And I from three days' peace.

Was it so hard, Achilles,
So very hard to die?
Thou knowest and I know not —
So much the happier I.

I will go back this morning
From Imbros over the sea:
Stand in the trench, Achilles,
Flame-capped and shout for me."

Annette sniffed. "It's just as well for his reputation as a poet that he was killed. Nobody otherwise would have thought much of *that.*"

For a moment he felt that he would like to throw her down the mountain. He turned away and said nothing. But he felt she was watching him, and when she spoke it was on a more serious note. "I'm sorry, Teddy boy. It means something to you, doesn't it? I shouldn't have been so flippant."

"No, you're perfectly right. It's not a good poem. Just a piece of doggerel, really."

"And maybe this war *is* something we all need. To think of Huns goose-stepping down the Champs Élysées. Ugh! I guess it's high time I *did* something with my life. What have I done in the four years since I came out but take courses in art and buy hats? And what do I do up here but scurry down to the swimming club at noon to see if Lex Shannon won't look at me?"

Ted glanced at her now as if in reluctant reappraisal. She certainly had an intellect that she was wasting. With a touch here and a twist there, with a little more weight and a little more happiness, she might have been conceived of as the potential hostess of some distinguished salon, "influencing" important men. Had it not been for her parentally deplored crush on Shannon, the handsome pianist who accompanied the quartet which played at noon at the club, he might almost have been in love with her himself. But such things were not to be thought of now.

"Maybe you could be a spy. A modern-day Mata Hari."

"That's right. Laugh at me. Because I didn't like your poem."

"I'm sorry. It's just that you don't have my problem."

"But what *is* your problem?"

"Let's start down the mountain," he said

gruffly and jumped up to lead the way.

She, of course, he reflected bitterly as they silently descended the slope, would have a lovely war. Exalted, inspired, she would sell War Bonds or raise money for the Red Cross, standing erect with tear-filled eyes in crowded hotel ballrooms as the national anthem was played under a flag rippled by artificial wind. Bliss was it in that dawn to be alive, but to be a woman, what heaven!

"Maybe global conflict will get you over Lex," he flung over his shoulder.

"Or throw him in my arms," she riposted with a laugh.

"That's right! If he goes to war and comes home a hero, your family can't object."

"Ah, but *he* may. If he won't look at me now, why should he then?"

Ted didn't tell her what everybody knew: that the beautiful Lex had the gall to be looking for a larger fortune than the depleted one of the Simpsons. Games; they were all playing games. Annette's broken heart would be easily glued.

At the bottom of the mountain they found his car, and he drove her home and then took himself to the village to see if there was any late news of the bombing of London. Walking up the main street of Bar Harbor from the swimming club, where he had parked, he imagined himself passing through one of those tin hamlets sold for stations for boys' railroad trains.

The street started at the docks amid the screams of a hundred wheeling gulls, rising to divide the little shops for a mile before it escaped to the woods and summer cottages and the grey-topped mountains. Nature and commerce blended in the beauty of careful maintenance. There was no tarnish to the sparkle of the sunshine, no blemish in the sky's cerulean blue. The glass in all the windows was spotless, and the stores themselves were freshly painted in diverse bright colors. Even the automobiles, cared for by chauffeurs, were shiny; he noted a green Rolls Royce touring car, a yellow Hispano limousine. It was hard to think of the shops as not always prospering, of the little old ladies in white or black, with straw hats, ever being unable to purchase the wares on their packed shelves.

But wasn't it all unreal, Ted asked himself, in what was becoming a habit of exasperation. Yes, but was it any more unreal than himself? It might be a smug, passive little world, but hadn't it some of the ineluctable force of the rocks along the seacoast which rebuffed the waves and turned them into great cascades of spray? It was a universe of the old; it knew it would be protected. It was also a woman's world. He even imagined some great rounded Greek statue of Ceres or Athena watching over it. Perhaps it had to send annual sacrifices to a Minotaur on another island, a remote island; but it could afford them. Young men and women? No, just young men. At least one young man.

Why, he asked himself impatiently, was he afflicted with this obsession? Did the photographs of his smiling young father, who could have had no sense of a shortened life line, seem to require it of him? No, be happy, they appeared to tell him. Yet as a boy had he not often caught himself peering apprehensively in the mirror for signs of a maturity which would mark the limits of his exemption? Had he not been made uneasy by the innocent compliments of aunts: "You're really quite the young man now, aren't you, dear?" He had even once consulted a psychiatrist, who related his reluctance to grow up, to turn into a man, to a fear of castration and asked him if as a child he had not caught sight of his half-sisters in the bath and noted what they didn't have and wondered who had cut it off. But boys who subconsciously dreaded the shearing off of their genitals were apt to try to postpone puberty by dressing as and acting like girls. He, on the contrary, had always gone in for violent sports, even playing football at Harvard, which none of his prep school crowd had.

Hadn't he been preparing himself for battle?

At the stationer's there was no further war news.

2

On the long shady veranda of the long dark shingle house on the Shore Path, whose two wings extended from a central tower, he found his stepfather, a Scotch and soda in hand, reading the market news. Gilbert Warner's smile was warmly welcoming. He made no secret of the fact that he had always wanted a son, and his preference for Ted over his own two daughters was embarrassingly obvious. With those vivacious female teen-agers he was jovial, joking, benignantly sarcastic; with their and Ted's mother he was courteous and elaborately gallant; but with Ted a rare note of sincerity seemed to be struck.

"I hope you're in for dinner. We have the Palmers coming. Their beautiful daughter will eradicate the silly Miss Simpson from your dreams and leave her to her vulgar bandmaster."

"Sorry, Gil. I'm due at the Musgraves' camp."

Warner's face clouded. "Of course, I cannot hope to compete with the mighty Musgrave. If you spurned my humble brokerage house to sit at his feet, how could I rival his hospitality? Still, I wonder, had you seen fit to join me in Wall Street, if you wouldn't have met in the flesh characters as colorful as any you could only read about in his Jacobean dramas."

"And as wicked?"

"Oh, I hope so. We must have our amusement somehow. I simply wonder that you prefer yours in books."

Ted sighed. What a paradise a future of books would be! He contemplated the handsome, hawklike countenance of his stepfather, the gleaming dome under a receding hairline, the chiseled features, the grey, investigating eyes. It struck him that he and Warner were like two contrasting Toby jars on a mantel, he too boyishly pleasant not to conceal melancholy and his stepfather too clever-looking not to be a bit of an ass. People didn't really respect Gilbert. Ted had always known that. His colorful sport coats and gleaming white flannels, his glittering foreign cars, his expertise at golf and bridge, his gallantry with the ladies and his witty repartée only intensified

Bar Harbor's suspicion that he was sharp, slick, a man who quit the bridge table when he was ahead and gypped the broker out of his commission on his many Mount Desert Island real estate deals. It was noticed that though he was quick to apply for scholarships in his daughters' schools in a bad year, he never cut down on his cars or his parties. No one could imagine why the sober, silent Amelia Atwood had married him.

"Well, anyway," Ted continued, shrugging, "Wall Street or Musgrave, it's not going to matter much now, is it?"

"How do you mean?"

"I know you and Ma think we ought to stay out of the war, but how long can we?"

"Please make a distinction between your mother and me. She deems it her duty, single-handedly if necessary, to stand between global conflict and her darling son so that not one hair of his pretty head shall be touched. While I naturally share this concern, I have other and broader grounds for my position."

"I know you think we've done enough for Britain."

"In the way of blood, yes. As you know, I didn't get abroad in the last war, but that wasn't my fault, I was in uniform and ready to go when it ended. We did our best, and we did enough. What England's basically trying to do is hang on to an empire she's too small to handle. Let her do it if she can, and good luck to her. And I'm happy to send her all the aid she wants. But let her pay for it. On credit, of course. Call me a war profiteer if you like. I've made a good thing out of arms industries, and I'm not ashamed of it. I lost a good job in the last war and never got it back. It's time war did something for me."

Ted almost wanted to be convinced that Gilbert was as bad as he sounded. Wouldn't it be preferable to believe that the dull peace, the banal charm of this static summer island were not all they added up to, but that underneath there might glint some of the fire and lust and wickedness that England's great poet dramatists had attributed to the Italy of their inflamed imaginations? Wouldn't it be more exciting to see his stepfather as a Vindice, a Bosola, a Flamineo, a remorseless villain, than as the fatuously self-excusing gainer from a lost but noble cause?

But no, no, he must stop letting his mind jump and tumble.

"You don't think there are greater issues at stake?" he asked.

"You mean like democracy? Or Hitler's treatment of the Jews? Nobody's keeping England from being democratic. And if they really cared about the Jews, they'd have done something about them years ago."

Ted saw that it was hopeless. "Let's not argue about it. Each man has to do his own thing. I believe we're going to get into this war. And if we don't, pretty soon, I know I'm going to."

His stepfather's groan showed that he had been expecting something like this. "How?"

"I might go to Montreal and sign up with the RCAF. I've two friends who are talking about that. And all those flying lessons I took last summer ought to pay off."

"Do you want to kill your mother?"

Ted rose and walked to the edge of the veranda and stared out at the prickly green pimple of an island known as Porcupine. Was he, Ted Atwood, another character in an Elizabethan drama, a Hamlet, a Philaster, the sole dark brooding member of a glittering carefree court, yearning to drown its garish falseness in the well of his truth? Or what he *deemed* its falseness and what he *deemed* his truth?

"I shouldn't have brought it up. Nothing's decided, anyway. And now I should be changing to go to the Musgraves'."

His stepfather rose at this, and Ted could see that he was suddenly angry. He had the pursed lips and stifled look of a man who knows he is going to say something that he is bound to regret.

"No doubt you will find the atmosphere in the professor's camp purer than in our depraved and worldly community. But there is one thing that Mr. Musgrave's Boswell, which I suppose is the role to which you aspire, will have to face. Why did such a fiery old Joe accept with such docility his wife's flagrant infidelities?"

"I didn't know he had."

"Oh, dear, yes. Margaret Musgrave, admirable lady that she is, took little pains to cover her traces. There's nothing of the hypocrite in *her,* anyway."

Why, Ted wondered, was Gilbert quite so anxious to deprive him of an idol? And why did he think this information would have that result? Did he realize how much his war attitude lowered him in his stepson's eyes, and wish now to besmirch anything the younger man *did* admire?

"I suppose you think I'm relaying some kind of dirty gossip" — Gilbert was apprehensive at his stepson's silence — "but my information is from an impeccable source. If you *must* know, I myself, as a lusty youth, enjoyed the favors of the lovely Maggie."

"*Must* I know?"

"They say the professor must have done something — or *not* done something — that deprived him of the right to take exception to her amorous flights. That he was impotent, or even that he may have inflicted her with a disease that was a relic of his bachelor days."

"I'd better be on my way, Gil. I'm really not terribly interested in Mrs. Musgrave's love life."

Gilbert reached out an appealing hand. "But it *is* better to know these things, don't you agree?"

3

The Musgraves' "camp" in Seal Cove, discreetly remote from the more fashionable centers of Bar and Northeast Harbors, consisted of a vast, comfortable log cabin, filled with quilted rugs and overstuffed divans, with formidable animal heads and navigational charts, and three guest cabins. Margaret Musgrave, a tall, handsome, rather stately lady with a small, perennial, quizzical smile, was the daughter of an early summer pioneer of the island, a minor railway tycoon whose heavy stone mansion atop a hill in Bar Harbor was still occupied by his son. But Margaret had preferred to establish an independent society "of the mind" and to entertain the intelligentsia of Mount Desert in her more rustic quarters, holding out the carrot of her scholarly consort.

The professor, who now waved a welcoming arm to Ted from his little circle of admiring younger males by the huge stone fireplace, had a fine square face, thick tousled grey hair, broad shoulders, bushy eyebrows and pale blue eyes which seemed to be looking through his interlocutor to something more significant or at least more amusing. At his wife's constant parties, which he disingenuously professed to despise, he loved to play the ham, thunderously proclaiming whatever opinions seemed least expected of his profundity, as, for example, that an evening at the bridge table was preferable to a conversation with Voltaire, that a successful writer of who-done-its was more to be envied than the most learned scholar or that the greatest comfort of old age might be to become a burden to ungrateful children.

Ted, approaching the group, found the great man engaged in a scatological discourse. "Ted, my boy, perhaps you can help us with the problem at hand. Mr. Tomkins here spoke of the Duce as kissing Herr Hitler's ass. I noted that this is the common phrase to describe the habitual action of toadies. But nobody here has been able to cite a factual example of any man actually kissing another man's ass. I am counting on my brilliant new aide to supply us with one."

Happily, Ted was a constant reader of Saint-Simon. "I can indeed, sir. The duc de Vendôme, when commanding the armies of Louis the Fourteenth in north Italy, had the unpleasant habit of receiving envoys while sitting on his close-stool. It was sometimes difficult for the Italian princes to induce their legates to put up with this. The duke of Parma, however, knew that his ambitious Alberoni would accept *anything*. When that wily diplomat was ushered into the presence of the odoriferous general, he went even further than required. When Vendôme rose, having completed his evacuations, Alberoni cried, '*O culo di angelo!*' and stumbled forward to press his lips against it."

Musgrave crowed in sheer delight. "Like Herod, Teddy boy, I offer you anything in my kingdom! Whose head will you have on a salver? But tell me. Was this Alberoni rewarded for his heroic stooping?"

"It was the start of his great career. As first minister of Spain, he controlled the destiny of Europe."

Musgrave rose now and embraced Ted, but when he was seated again it was clear that the subject had been exhausted. He turned to the war.

"I'm sure you're for our getting into it, aren't you, sir?" Ted asked.

"Are you so sure, my lad, are you?" The great bushy eyebrows soared as if to reach the imponderable. "It certainly seems as if the Hun is determined on the destruction of all that is most precious in our culture. Imagine bombs raining down on our beloved London!" The great head shook sadly. "Yet it sometimes seems to me that it may even be our painful duty to keep out of this mortal conflict, if only to preserve the arts and graces which may serve a ravaged world to rebuild its civilization. It would be hard, I know, for brave young men like you to stand by while so much of what we all love and admire goes up in flames, but it *could* be the higher obligation."

"Would you feel that way, sir, if you were my age?"

"Ah, that's it, that's it," the older man exclaimed, rather too stagily, even for him. "I shall never know, shall I? I have always wondered whether I should be a hero or a poltroon in war. And if I were a young man today and took the position I have just taken, mightn't my real motive be to save my own pelt? And might that not still be my motive, to cast a kind of consistency over a long lifetime of hidden fear?"

Ted thought of his stepfather's gossip. Was the old man's self-laceration a false shame for his sexual impotence, or a tedious and banal male preoccupation with the eternal question of untested courage? Had the great belligerent issues of past and present dwindled in his self-absorption to imagined gauges of Charles Musgrave's virility? The group around the fireplace had widened; more guests had arrived, including several ladies. Ted slipped off to look for his hostess. But why, he wondered, did he care so much about the war attitudes of people he would leave behind when he succumbed to his compulsion to be drawn into the conflict? Wasn't it easier to feel that he was ridding himself of a world indifferent to foreign sacrifice, intent on its own little games and profits, a world that saw the ordeal of England at most as an exciting drama, at least as the fall of a superannuated power? And yet he hated to see it that way. If he was to die, he wanted to die like his poet soldier, with Achilles shouting for him, leaving a world which, like Britain in 1915, was well aware that Rupert Brooke was dead in Scyros.

Mrs. Musgrave was also looking for him. "I've put you next to Miss Gwen Howard at table. I think you'll like her. She's a sporty old English type who's been in their embassy forever. Try to take her mind off London.

Poor thing, she's frantic about it."

Miss Howard was already at her seat when he went in. Her figure was long and thin, too thin, her nose long, pointed and distinguished, her eyes huge and dark, and her black hair (presumably dyed as she had to be well over fifty) was loosely wavy and tied in a tight knot behind. He made a polite reference to the British legation in Washington.

"Oh, yes, I've been there twenty years. And you may well ask why I'm not there now. I should indeed be, and at my desk around the clock, but I had a nasty bout with pneumonia, and our dear ambassador, who was kind enough to attribute it to overwork, absolutely ordered me to take a month's rest. And as my old friend Margaret insisted that I come up here, here I am! Though it's hard to rest in these days. For a Brit, anyway."

"Perhaps Mount Desert Island is the only place where it's even conceivable."

"Because it's not quite real? But in some ways, don't you think, that can make it worse?"

"Oh, I know what you mean!" He was suddenly intensely excited, and he had to be silent for a moment to get his feelings under control. He was certain that he was going to like this old girl. "Tell me what you do at the embassy."

"Well, what I'm supposed to be is a kind of social secretary. But my real function is to take the blame. Suppose, for example, we've given a dinner party for our visiting poet laureate, and the plan was to keep it more or less literary. And then one of your, shall we say, less erudite Western senators complains that he wasn't invited and that his wife, who has literary pretensions, is much miffed. Our chief will take him aside and confide in him, 'I'm sorry, old fellow, but you see we're stuck with this old dragon, Miss Howard. She's some dim kin, I believe, to the duke of Norfolk and is supposed to have pull with one of the royals. She does her job on the whole pretty well, but she's still capable of the most horrible boo-boos. At that party for the laureate an odd little man with your surname, whom nobody knew, turned up and got wretchedly squiffed. Dear old Howard had got her lists mixed again!' " She paused as Ted laughed. "I *am* a very distant and obscure cousin of the dear duke, but I have no royal protection, and I *don't* make boo-boos. But I'm only too happy to be useful to my beleaguered country in any way my superiors see fit. After all, I can't fight."

He looked at her admiringly. "But you would if you could."

"Would I! Ah, yes what a joy to die in such

a cause! But dying may not be necessary. We're going to win, you know. I was thrilled by that statement of Paul Reynaud. Do you remember it? 'If I were told that only a miracle could save France, then I believe in miracles, for I believe in France.' Don't look at me that way, young man. I know that miracle was not forthcoming. Not at that time. But it *will* come, if necessary, for England, and *that* will ultimately save France. So Reynaud was right, you see."

He was struck by the strange gleam in her dark eyes. Was she a bit of a fanatic?

"Were you here in the other war?"

"Oh, no, I came over afterwards. I lost my fiancé, Tommy Currier. Gassed at the Somme. Poor Tommy, he never had a groat, no more did I, and we foolishly put off marrying until the war should be over. After the Armistice I wanted to get away as far as possible, which is why I came here."

"Tell me what it was like in England before 1914. Did you feel the war coming? Was there foreboding in the air?"

"None at all." She shook her head serenely. "We look back on those days now as the golden twilight of an empire. But we had no idea that it *was* a twilight. All those great house parties! It was a heady, lavish time. Maybe it was all vanity, but I'm glad I saw it. We were poor Howards, but how we clung to the fringes!"

"Did you know Patrick Shaw-Stewart?"

"Bless me, how do you know about him? Indeed, I did know him, and the Grenfell brothers, and I even met Rupert Brooke! All those beautiful doomed young men! A whole unmatchable generation lost! I remember my father, who was a don at Oxford, saying, with a sigh, about a class of young men physically disqualified for the army, 'I see now the meaning of the phrase *mens sana in corpore sano.*' "

"At least those who served had happiness in their prewar life. They didn't know what was coming."

"Unlike our poor chaps today who grew up under the shadow of Hitler? That's true. But can't there still be exhilaration in watching the devil grow into the fiend you can destroy?"

At this point he had to let her talk to her loquacious host on the other side, and she couldn't turn back to him before the meal was over. After dinner he sat with Mrs. Musgrave in the living room. He waxed enthusiastic about Miss Howard.

"Yes, I noticed you with her. You seemed very intent. What was it all about? England's finest hour, and all that?"

Ted was so shocked he could hardly speak for a moment. Then he said, solemnly, "I found her inspiring."

She smiled with a benignity little in keeping with her words. "I see you find me trivial. Or perhaps heartless. But it's not that. It's simply that I deplore the shrill heroism of the noncombatant."

"But Miss Howard does all she can for her country!"

"I don't doubt it. But it isn't much, is it? Let her be more quiet."

"How can she be quiet when her countrymen are being blown to bits?"

"Her countrymen? My dear Ted, the unfortunate folk being killed in the raids are probably with one or two exceptions, no closer to her than to you or me. They're English, yes, but so are we by descent. The point is they're human beings, and human beings are always being slaughtered in one part or another of the globe. Should we live in a perpetual state of horror and indignation? And how would that help anyone?"

"So you think we should sit smugly and do nothing?"

"I didn't say we had to be smug. Though much as I love dear Gwen, I think she *is* a bit smug about her depth of caring. I see I'm putting you out of temper. That's all right. Indignation is becoming to your youthful looks. No, I think people should do whatever they think it's right for them to do. But while they're not engaged in doing it, they shouldn't wail and preach. They should continue to cultivate the good life, wherever they happen to be. It seems to me just as idle to wring your hands over distant misery as over past misery. Should we be weeping because some of our ancestors were scalped by redskins?"

"London seems a lot closer to me than Indian massacres."

"Then *do* something about it if you must, but in the meantime, my young friend, *carpe diem!* Don't be a bleeding heart, like poor Gwen."

"But think, Mrs. Musgrave, what she's been through! Losing the one man she ever loved in the last war."

"The *one* man, exactly. She preferred to sit by the monument, 'smiling at grief,' rather than bestir herself to find another. There's a kind of pleasure in that, I suppose. It's never been one that *I've* gone in for."

Ted's indignation had now been replaced by something akin to awe. Who was this aging Helen of Troy? What was it to her that silly males should wrangle over her beauty? "The professor implied that if he were a young man, he might want to go over and fight for the British."

"He can say that because he's not a young man."

Ted was embarrassed to be caught in his tergiversation. "You think it was an idle boast?"

"Of course it was an idle boast! Really, you men can make awful fools of yourselves. Like two bull moose fighting over a cow instead of taking turns. I'm honestly glad that I was born a woman. Though I admit we have our fools, too. Like poor Gwen. Well, at least I never made *her* mistake."

Ted stared silently at his hostess, unable to think what to retort to this. But other guests now joined them. The conversation turned to the war, and the Versailles treaty was blamed for it. When Mrs. Musgrave exclaimed, with a laugh, "We fought to get rid of the Kaiser, and what wouldn't we give to have *him* back in Berlin?" he rose abruptly and walked out to the porch to gaze at the stars.

What a terrible woman! Might it not have been *she* who had castrated the professor? Who could have made love to her but a man like his stepfather, who believed in nothing but himself and shared her immunity to the sentimental appeal of senseless slaughter, senseless heroism and senseless pity?

He felt a presence behind him. Miss Howard had followed him out.

"I want to go on with our talk," she said. "We hadn't finished, had we? And I like you so much." She just touched his elbow. It gave him a sudden thrill.

"It must be awful for you to be up here with all these silly people!" he exclaimed excitedly. "Listening to all their rot about the war!"

"I don't really mind that. The only thing I mind is when I suspect one of them of believing that England is going down. Oh, they never say it, of course. They even quote Winston. But I can always tell." He turned to her in surprise, feeling that her gaze, even in the darkness, was reproachful. "Yes, my friend, *you* are one of those doubters. You are different because you care so deeply. You want to go down with us. But you still think that's going to happen. Aren't I right?"

"The German power *is* appalling," he muttered. "I can't help thinking of what happened to France."

"But we're not France. Come over to the window, my friend, where you can see my eyes in the light." He followed her obediently. She turned back to him now, and he stared into those fixed, dark orbs. "Can you look at me and *not* see that we are bound to win?"

He looked and looked and he saw no such thing. But he saw something else. He saw

1915. He saw Scyros and Rupert Brooke. He saw or thought he saw that she was giving him something that would make a kind of sense out of his obsession. It might be all that he needed; it wasn't too much; it might be just enough, but he would have to act on it hastily before it vanished into the magic and treacherous air of the island.

"I *do* see it," he lied happily. "Thank you, dear Miss Howard!"

4

Amelia Warner's white-cheeked, placid countenance was turned to the restless blue-grey water between Porcupine Island and her veranda. Her stillness, her air of remoteness, her grey-haired composure were at odds with the windy day, the wheeling gulls, the busy pleasure boats. Her earnest visitor could hardly be sure she was even listening. Miss Howard bent intently forward in her wicker chair as she talked.

"I have been tortured, Mrs. Warner, ever since I got that letter from Montreal which I sent you. When I didn't hear from you, I simply had to come. Of course, I see his enlisting as an absolutely heroic thing. But I know of your stand against intervention. I quite see that you may resent me passionately."

"It would be quite understandable," Amelia replied calmly, after a pause. She continued to gaze out over the water. "But now that he's actually gone, now that there's nothing I can do about it, I feel a certain passivity. There doesn't seem to be any particular place in me for resentment. You seem to have cut the last faint strand of his umbilical cord. I suppose it was about to part, anyway."

"You understand, I hope, that I never suggested that he do anything like this?"

"I speak of the *effect* of what you said, Miss Howard, not the particular words. There was no reason you should not have expressed yourself as you did on a subject about which you cared so strongly."

"Oh, I'm so glad you see it that way! I do feel that this terrible war is the whole world's business. Perhaps now that your son is in it, you will feel that all America should come to back him up."

"No, Miss Howard, I don't feel that at all. I simply feel that there is nothing further for me to do about the question, one way or the other."

"But surely you must feel involved now!"

Mrs. Warner shook her head firmly. "I don't blame you for not understanding me. We have only just met, and I am not a person you would have been likely to come across in your life. Let me explain some things — since our paths have so oddly crossed. I was one of those who were deeply disillusioned by the last war. I had seen it initially as the war to end wars and all that. I acquiesced completely with my first husband when he decided to enlist. We both felt, though I was a dependent and an expectant mother, that he should not claim deferment. When he was killed, and the Allies threw away at Versailles everything he had died for, I made a pledge to myself that I would keep his son alive at all costs. I would stand between him and everything that threatened his life. I married again, largely to have an ally in my determination. But I failed from the beginning. I had only to frown on violent sport, and he would go in for it, even playing football right through college, unlike any of his friends. If I so much as looked at a mountain, he would climb it. If I shuddered at the sea, he would join a trans-Atlantic sailing race. I began to feel that my precautions were magnets drawing him into risks he would not otherwise have taken. You need feel no guilt, Miss Howard.

He was bound to find you. He may even have been looking for you. His library was full of books on the last war. You seem to have been the green light he was waiting for."

"He will come back to you, Mrs. Warner! He will come back to you a victorious hero, and we shan't make the old mistakes of Versailles again!"

"Perhaps not. But there will be plenty of others for us to make."

"Oh, my dear Mrs. Warner, is there *nothing* you believe in?"

Ted's mother rose now and, without taking any leave or further notice of her visitor, she walked to the edge of the veranda, stepped down to the lawn and proceeded slowly to the rocks by the water.

When Gwen Howard rose to depart she saw that her hostess appeared to have settled herself on a wooden bench for the remainder of the afternoon.

Priestess and Acolyte

1

I am constantly urged to write my memoirs, but I have always declined. Publishers and friends and literary agents are always after me to reveal "the woman behind the actress," the "real" Adrienne Toland. The very plainness and simplicity of my public image in these turbulent nineteen-seventies, as a diffident, spinsterish, almost venerable lady, puts to rout even the notion of past lovers, unless, of course, there should have been an appropriately dead hero in the First World War or some dim shade of a man who was not "free." This naturally excites the curiosity of those who, not illogically, associate theatrical fame with romance, or rather romanc*es,* and plenty of them, at that. Wasn't there an essential contradiction between the picture of what (if unlabeled) might have been a beloved old high school teacher, or even the paid companion of some rich octogenarian invalid, and the glittering theatre on Broadway now rechristened The Adrienne Toland? *Cherchez l'homme!* Or even *la femme,* in these days of relaxed sexual standards. But at least give them *somebody*. Didn't even the ethereal Duse have her D'Annunzio?

But I am determined to preserve this image which I have built up so long and with such painstaking care. When I was in the hospital recently with what turned out to be a benign but hard-to-diagnose infection, I was asked by a young resident doctor if I had ever had a baby. I replied, "Young man, if you will take the trouble to look at the top of my chart, you will see that it reads *Miss* Toland." There! Doesn't that give you the picture? Well, that, if I have anything to do with it, is the picture which will last my time. And after that I can hardly care.

The only reason, then, that I have decided to write this private memoir is to try to explain myself to myself. That it will be the true answer to what people insist on seeing as my "enigma" I cannot guarantee. We are all fallible, especially about ourselves. But it may interest some people to learn how *I* saw the enigma. Or wanted to see it. If I think well of the piece when it is finished, I may bequeath it to my dear cousin Nora. She can do with it as she sees fit.

Very well. So, on with it.

From early childhood I have entertained a passion for everything about the theatre but the actors themselves. Let me say at once that I must have been a fairly hateful child, for I secretly despised my poor parents. Yet even today as I try to look back on them with some dispassion, I find them exasperating. My father, Lionel Toland, over forty when I was born, had been in his prime a famous star of repertory, but he had foolishly persisted in stretching out his career into an alcoholic old age, overplaying Shylock, Richelieu and Cyrano to sadly diminishing audiences. To me he exemplified the worst of thespian traits. His stage and home emotions were so inextricably blended that I never knew, in my teens, whether I was Cordelia to a cursing Lear or Little Eva to an adoring St. Clare. And my mother, Winifred Allen, a tall, throaty, noble Portia or Imogene on the boards, also imbibed, though in private and not nearly so much as her spouse. She never convinced *me* when she solemnly maintained that theatre folk were the most loyal, loving and generous people in the world, knowing as I did that she would buss on both cheeks and address piercingly as "dahling, dahling" a person whom she had vilified atrociously only an hour before. As a family, my parents, brother and I, and here and there an uncle or aunt, were always on tour. We never saw any but theatre people or discussed anything but theatre matters. For us, all the world really was a stage. Seen from the orchestra pit we might have had a dash of color or romance, but from the wings it was all paint and fustian.

There had never been any question but that I too should tread the boards. I lacked the dark good looks of my brother, who my family insisted would one day be a matinée idol; my face was pale and round and undramatic, and my hair sandy and straight. But my eyes were all right, large, pale blue and capable of steady gazing — Father always said he could "do" something with my eyes — and I could remember a surprising number of lines after a single reading. Also, I had a clear, carrying voice. It was thought that I might be trained for character parts, but after my success at age twelve as Arthur in *King John* to my mother's Constance, Father decided that I need not be so limited, and in my teens I moved on to Nerissa and Charmian. "If I can make her an actress, she can make herself beautiful," he would say, with that loyalty to the cliché which abounds in the profession. If I have done anything, it is to prove that beauty is *not* a necessity to stardom.

I had accepted as my at least temporary home base the fantasy world of my parents with an outward docility which masked my inner dissent from all but the most discerning.

Theatre people are apt to be discerning only in the agility with which they pick up the mannerisms of persons whom they wish to mimic; their art does not require them to penetrate the surface. Father and Mother saw no reason to suspect that my placidly undemonstrative manner covered anything but the properest filial devotion. And I, imagining their world to be a strong one — strong so far as my impoverished and plain self was concerned — was resigned to go along with it until I should find some trustworthy and (I cared enough for them to hope) tactful escape to a better one.

I knew, anyway, that I was not wasting my time. Repertory is the best possible training for an actor. But my concept of our profession was loftier than my parents': I saw in it the power of eliciting some ultimate beauty from paint and pantomine; I deemed it the only key to the fullest appreciation of our greatest poets and playwrights. Indeed, I could sometimes almost forgive my family the vulgarity of their melodramatic interpretations of certain roles in the light of what I suspected were their occasional glimpses of the ideals that informed my soul. But for the most part I was nothing if not critical. When they took me to see the aging Sarah Bernhardt in *Phèdre* and *L'Aiglon* and raved over the famous *voix d'or,* I could only hide my conviction that for all her genius she was basically a ham.

It was only when I saw Eleanora Duse in *La Città Morta* that I knew my private ideal was attainable. That she wore no makeup exalted me; it seemed the ultimate justification of my hatred of the "show" in show business. The great actress was then in the last year of her life, but my vision of her was Amy Lowell's:

Seeing you stand once more before my
 eyes
In your pale dignity and tenderness,
Wearing your frailty like a misty dress
Draped over the great glamour which
 denies

To years their domination, all disguise
Time can achieve is but to add a stress,
A finer idleness as though some caress
Touched you a moment to a strange
 surprise.

It was in that same year, 1923, that my withdrawal from my parents' company was occasioned, not by my flight, as I had come to dread it might have to be, but by its own collapse. Father's drinking had grown worse and worse, and it finally resulted in the breakdown of one of his performances. He was playing the wicked but epigrammatic Lord Illingworth in Wilde's *A Woman of No Importance*, and I was the prim American heiress, Hester, in love with Gerald Arbuthnot, who was, unknown to all but his mother, Illingworth's bastard son. It was a part which I had sought to make sympathetic by giving a noble rather than a censorious ring to her speeches on America's moral superiority to Britain, but I was sadly put off by Father's condition. In the scene where I rush on stage, fleeing Lord Illingworth's attempted embraces, which the director had chosen to place in a garden, Father, lustily in pursuit, was supposed to fling open the gate which I had slammed behind me. But it wouldn't open, at least not to his clumsy fumbling. He turned suddenly to the audience and shouted, "Damn it all, I hope someday I'll get a stage manager who can make things open when they're supposed to!"

He then marched offstage. When the gate was opened by a stagehand, and Father returned, the climactic scene where Gerald moves to strike him and is stopped by his mother, crying, "Don't, don't, he's your father!" was obviously ruined.

While Father and Mother were ineffectively trying to reconstitute their shattered company, they could hardly blame me for marketing my talents elsewhere, particularly as my new field in no way competed with them. I had decided to try my fortune as a monologuist.

My motivation must be obvious from what I have already written about my chaste view of the art of the theatre. Alone on a bare stage, free of scenery and other actors, I had hoped to realize something of my acting ideals. Were not those the conditions to activate my imagination to its highest pitch? But my first trouble was that there was no literature of monologues; each artist in the field, usually a woman, had written her own. Secondly, it was an art that lends itself primarily to comedy. I did manage to write six passable sketches of famous American women (Mary Lincoln and Emily Dickinson were the two best), and my agent arranged a fairly successful tour across the country, mostly to women groups, but I gave up this new career when my brother, Lester, who had finally induced Father to retire and had reactivated the family company, persuaded me to "come home" and try things again under his more beneficent management. His clinching argument was that I had invaded a field which had room for only one great star, Ruth Draper.

Lester was far the best of all our family, cousins included, and the only one I really loved. He was strangely free of the egotism of our profession. He had beautiful pale dark looks which had rapidly made him a romantic star, but they were partly the product of infected lungs which brought him to an early grave. His production of *Hedda Gabler*, in which he had the generosity to cast me in the lead and himself in the lesser role of Lövberg, made my name, and when I sat by his death bed, only a year later, he grasped my hand with his weak one and murmured, "Keep at it, Sis. You have it made if you'll only do it *your* way. You'll compensate for the whole damn family."

Well, keep at it I did. I took what he meant by "my way" as a dying command. *My* way was to commit myself as a kind of vestal virgin to the altar of art. He knew that I had never had a lover, and I believe that *he* believed his own very opposite conduct in that area had weakened his performances and hastened his demise. In my period of mourning I solemnly vowed, not only to preserve all my energies for my art, but to act only in dramas worthy of my dedication to it.

I have kept that vow. I have never appeared in a play, old or new, that I have not chosen myself. And I have rigidly kept my life offstage as a service department to my life on. My friends have been few but close, usually but not always women, and rarely from the theatre world; my vacations, when not spent in travel, have been quiet ones on my Vermont farm, full of reading and gardening; my charities have been largely in the education of my less well off but numerous younger relations.

I have had a public, of course, and I have found it expedient to develop a public personality. I had to learn how to satisfy the press with interviews that would convince them they had enough and could leave me alone for a while. I was "gracious" with reporters, modest, amiable and very polite. My statements were just dull enough to keep them from wanting to come back without giving them the suspicion that I was "holding out" on them. Ultimately they accepted at face value the picture of a nice old maid who had given all to her roles and had nothing left to give anyone else.

And wasn't it true? Hadn't the image become a reality? It was to be tested only once.

2

At forty-two, at the height of my career, with six distinguished Broadway hits behind me, I received a letter which considerably startled me. I had never been to Hollywood, or even considered appearing in a film — mine was not a face for close-ups, and besides, I thought little of the medium — but even I had heard of Tony Maddux, the "new young heartthrob of the silver screen," as he was denominated in *Variety*. And here is what I read:

Dear Miss Toland:

I have admired you passionately all my life.

Some might deem it ungallant of me so to expose the difference in our ages, but I know your mind is too lofty for such pettiness.

The success I have achieved is the vulgarest tinsel to the golden glow of your more merited fame.

My redemption, however, may lie in my awareness that my only chance of becoming a true actor lies on the boards and not in this fairyland of celluloid.

I have heard that you are planning a revival of *Candida.* Would you give me the chance to show you how I could play Marchbanks?

Oh, please, please, divine Miss Toland! This may be the major crisis of my life.

Yours in the ranks of death! Tony Maddux.

I showed this curious epistle to Peter Schenke, my producer, who was immediately intrigued.

"But the first thing we'll have to do is check out his drinking. He's supposed to be a terrible lush. That's not hopeless in films. If you're big enough box office, they can always arrange to shoot when you're sober. But can he meet a regular schedule of six nights and two matinées? Of course, he'd *look* the part to perfection. And his name, added to yours, would fill the house if we played *The Tale of Peter Rabbit.*"

Maddux certainly looked the part. I went that same day to see one of his films. Though the movie didn't show it, I had learned that he was on the short side, and his pale, thin, beautifully spectral face and haunting dark eyes gave him the air of a young Hamlet, still perhaps at Wittenberg, the kind of *jeune premier* who was irresistible to teen-age girls, sentimental mothers and homosexual men. It was also his reputation, as my realistic, untheatrical, favorite cousin, Nora Toland, was quick to inform me, that he was only too willing to share the bed of any person falling into one of those categories.

"Are you warning me?" I demanded. "I hardly fit."

"Well, you don't have to be a mother to feel the maternal urge. Besides, my dear, wouldn't a man like that regard your very impregnability as a challenge?"

"We must see first whether he's 'a man like that.' "

Peter Schenke's check with Hollywood friends having revealed that Maddux's drinking was not supposed to interfere with his work schedule, we invited him to come east for a conference. He came at once and announced dramatically at our first meeting that he had already bought his way out of his Hollywood contract. Before we had even engaged him! This turned out to be not quite true — some slipped-over details resulted in a lawsuit — but his zeal was contagious, his manners charming, and when he read the part, he was Marchbanks to the life. We engaged him for a fraction of the salary he could have obtained from anyone else, and rehearsals started.

Everyone interested in the theatre will remember that the 1940 production of *Candida* was a hit; some critics even wrote that Shaw might have written it for Tony and me. At the end of our limited engagement Tony, triumphant now on Broadway as well as in Hollywood, might have done anything he wanted, but he chose instead, as all his fans know, after making two disappointing films, to go the way of drink and drugs and at last the fatal overdose, only three years later. But my interest here is strictly confined to our relationship during our run on Broadway.

I played Candida as a woman of deep intelligence and mercilessly blunt speech who was too deeply aware of the loyalty she believed she owed her fatuous but high-minded husband to think anyone could take seriously her parlor flirtation with an emotionally exuberant young man. Yet I tried at the same time to convey a sense of the dark thoughts that must cross the mind of a woman who sees herself as a shuttlecock, to be batted to and fro between her prig of a spouse and a smart alec boy. Tony played Marchbanks in the liveliest fashion, getting the maximum audience reaction to the character's witticisms, but he added a greater degree of passion to the part than I could read in the text. His love was much more than that of a puppy.

Unfortunately, he elected to play this new Marchbanks off the boards as well as on. Alone with him, I would be extolled in hyperbole.

"Divine Miss Toland! You can't imagine — nobody *could* imagine — what it means to me to be with you, to gaze at you, to be rapt by you. Dare I call you Adrienne?"

At first I thought it was tact that curtailed these rhapsodies when he and I were in company, but I began at last to see that he was shrewd enough to understand that such an embarrassment might cause me to break off all personal relationship. What then did he want? What was he up to?

He would insist on taking me to lunch on non-matinée days at the most expensive restaurants in town, where he would pour forth the sad story of his early years: the much-wedded neglectful mother, the brute of a father, the loneliness of the only child, the humilities of genteel poverty, the cruelties of the military school, and then the sudden sweep to fame, the dizzying adulation, the false friends, the drinking, all the cheap tinsel of Hollywood stardom. That he chattered more about himself than about me was my fault. I turned away his eager questions about my own grey past. I much preferred to listen.

For I liked him. Oh, yes, I found myself liking him more and more. He was so warm, so charming, so "bright-eyed and bushy-tailed," like a cuddly spaniel, and, heavens, I was a woman, after all. Nora had been quite right to warn me. But I still didn't think I had to go so far as to make a resolution that I wasn't going to let things go any farther. Where could they go? Wouldn't there have been a kind of odious conceit in such a precaution?

That was it! Could anything so shiny, so golden, so lovely ever be attracted to an old bag whose magic went out as the curtain fell? There was no use in my indulging in fantasies of a young gallant flinging his cloak over a mud puddle to spare the slippers of the Virgin Queen — young gallants in Tudor days knew very well on which side their bread was buttered. And what did the all-popular Tony have to gain from me? But, on the other hand, was it utter folly to consider that he obviously had a neurotic yearning to be loved, and that the affection of a love-starved older woman (was *that* what I was coming to be?), intensified by feverish gratitude, might offer delights to such a man equal to those provided by his physical peers? If Tony was Eros, might not the love within himself create a love in his union with *any* partner on which the gods could smile?

But the moment I had faced the horrid fact that my reeling imagination was leading me into strange by-paths from which I might not be able to find a return, I began to ask myself if there was not something sinister in what was happening. Could there be something in the dark recesses of this young man's mind, something of which he himself might be totally unconscious, a lurking jealousy that made him seek to put out a light that was brighter than his own? If austerity and dedication had been the twin godparents of my art, might not that art be sapped in the warm baths of emotional indulgence that his eyes seemed constantly to suggest?

And then one day at lunch he really startled me. He asked me to marry him.

"Oh, my dear boy, what are you talking about?" I almost wailed in dismay. "How can you make such cruel fun of an old woman?"

"Forty-two is hardly old. And I've never been more serious in my life! We could be as great a team off the boards as on. You need someone to bring you out, to give you joy, to make you *live*. Right now you live only for your art. And I need your order and sanity and discipline. And we both need love. Oodles and oodles of love!"

"Tony, dear, be sensible. It would be grotesque! Besides, you need some fine young woman who could give you children. Which I couldn't at my age. At least I think I couldn't."

"Ah, there's a concession in your not thinking you could!" he exclaimed with a little shout of laughter. "It means you're considering my offer. Well, then, consider it! I can wait. And anyway we wouldn't need any children. You'd have quite enough with me!"

"No, no, it's impossible. Absolutely impossible."

"It's not!"

"It is, and you know it is." Here I spoiled everything by starting to weep. "This is too ludicrous. I'm going home." He got up when I did. "No, no, you stay here. I'll get my own cab."

"When will I see you?"

"At the theatre, of course."

"And after?"

"No! Only at the theatre. Please! From now on."

And I fled.

It was Friday. That night we performed as usual, but I refused to see him when he came to my dressing room door. The next morning, Phil Murray, an older actor who had known Tony in Hollywood and in whose brownstone he was staying, called me to say that Tony had come home late and very drunk the night before and that he thought I had better come around and help get him up if I wanted him in shape for the matinée.

"I've already tried once," he explained. "But I think I'm going to need someone with your authority."

I went to his house at once. Phil met me at the front door. "Why don't you go upstairs and see what you can do?" he suggested. "It's the third-floor back bedroom."

"Is he decent?"

"Well, he was covered up when I went in. He screamed at me to go away. Just call him from the doorway. I'll come right up if you need help."

But when I opened the door to Tony's room, I found him not covered up at all. He had thrown off his sheet and lay there on his back, fully exposed, in deep slumber. The shocking thing was that I didn't run away. No, I didn't. Instead, I approached the bed and stared at him. I might have been Psyche, raising the lamp to the forbidden sight of her unseen lover! Never will I forget that beautiful alabaster body. It reminded me of the statue of the nude drowned Shelley in University College in Oxford. My mind was in pieces. My mind was in flames.

But then he awakened. He stared at me for

a puzzled moment and then leaped from the bed.

"Adrienne! My love!"

He tried to embrace me, seemingly unaware of his state.

"Oh, for God's sake, look at you!" I cried. "Put something on!"

But he was quite unabashed. "Come to bed with me, dearest. I must have summoned you in my dream. Come!"

He grabbed me, but I struggled wildly and at last escaped. I ran down the stairs and out the front door, but not without shouting back to Phil to get him ready for the matinée. No, I could never forget *that*.

Two weeks later we closed, and Tony returned to Hollywood. He soon forgot me; I knew he would. He was not made for lasting affections. But I have been unable to keep from wondering at times whether, had I taken him up on his rash offer and actually married him, I might have kept him on a steadier path for a year or so before he left me for another woman — or man. And would I have lengthened his life by that short span? And would it have been worth it, for either of us? I doubt it. It was in his nature to corrupt and in mine to survive. And I *have* survived. But I daresay there are those who will think I haven't. And even, perhaps, that I shouldn't have.

The employees of THORNDIKE PRESS hope you have enjoyed this Large Print book. All our Large Print books are designed for easy reading — and they're made to last.

Other Thorndike Large Print books are available at your library, through selected bookstores, or directly from us. Suggestions for books you would like to see in Large Print are always welcome.

For more information about current and upcoming titles, please call or mail your name and address to:

THORNDIKE PRESS
PO Box 159
Thorndike, Maine 04986
800/223-6121
207/948-2962